I pushed the bottle down perch. Taking the cup from Meteor, I drifted to the hearth where Leona's coloured smoke swirled and danced. There I shook the cup, scattering a smidgen of powder.

The colours vanished, and the smoke with them. It didn't take any time; the smoke didn't die down. It simply ceased to be.

Dread slid through me, and I began to shake. The cup still held a pinch of powder; before I could drop it, I set it down on the hearthstones and flew backward. Turning to my friends, I found them bunched together, trembling.

'I wanted you to sprinkle that on *me*,' Leona whispered.

'It doesn't strengthen magic,' said Meteor. 'It *kills* magic. Probably kills any magical being too.'

Leona's silver eyes had turned grey with fright. 'It could have killed *me*.'

Also available by Victoria Hanley

Violet Wings

The Light of the Oracle
The Seer and the Sword

Indigo Magic

Victoria Hanley

CORGI BOOKS

INDIGO MAGIC
A CORGI BOOK 978 0 552 56235 5

First published in Great Britain by Corgi Books,
an imprint of Random House Children's Books
A Random House Group Company

This edition published 2012

1 3 5 7 9 10 8 6 4 2

The Random House Group Limited supports the Forest Stewardship
Council (FSC®), the leading international forest-certification organization.
Our books carrying the FSC label are printed on FSC®-certified paper.
FSC is the only forest-certification scheme endorsed by the leading
environmental organizations, including Greenpeace. Our paper-procurement
policy can be found at www.randomhouse.co.uk/environment.

MIX
Paper from
responsible sources
FSC® C016897

Set in Bembo

Corgi Books are published by Random House Children's Books,
61–63 Uxbridge Road, London W5 5SA

www.kidsatrandomhouse.co.uk
www.totallyrandombooks.co.uk
www.randomhouse.co.uk

Addresses for companies within The Random House Group Limited
can be found at: www.randomhouse.co.uk/offices.htm

THE RANDOM HOUSE GROUP Limited Reg. No. 954009

A CIP catalogue record for this book is available from the British Library.

Printed and bound by CPI Group (UK) Ltd, Croydon, CR0 4YY

TO THE ONGOING FRIENDSHIP
BETWEEN HUMANS AND FEY FOLK

Gremlin Territory

Iron La...

Leprechaun Colony

Palace of the Trolls

Troll Country

FE...

Pixandelle

Pixie's Meadow

N W E S

Glendonite Lake

Sapphire Stronghold

Anshield Island

...s

...e Ugly Mug

LAND

Gateway of Galena

Galena

Zaria's home

Oberon City

...aria's ...ortal

Tirfeyne

Chapter One

THE GLACIER SPELL IS ONE OF THE MOST FEARED IN FEYLAND, FOR GLACIER CLOTH FREEZES WHOMEVER IT TOUCHES — NOT AS WATER IS FROZEN INTO SOLID FORM: THE VICTIM OF THE SPELL IS FROZEN WITHIN TIME ITSELF.

THE PRINCESS WHO BECAME KNOWN AS 'SLEEPING BEAUTY' WAS WRAPPED IN GLACIER CLOTH. SHE DID NOT FIND THE EXPERIENCE UNPLEASANT, BUT SHE WAS A HUMAN, AFTER ALL. SHE DID NOT HAVE MAGIC OF HER OWN, BUT ONLY THE MANY GIFTS HEAPED UPON HER BY COMPETING GODMOTHERS. TO HER, THE YEARS SPENT FROZEN WOULD HAVE SEEMED MUCH LIKE A DREAM.

GLACIER CLOTH IS NOT AS KIND TO FEY FOLK. A FAIRY OR GENIE DOES NOT SLEEP BUT IS PRESERVED, AWAKE BUT UNABLE TO MOVE. MOST TRY TO FIGHT THE SPELL, BUT THIS IS OF NO USE.

FEW CAN PERFORM THE GLACIER SPELL, AND IT IS UNIQUE AMONG ENCHANTMENTS, FOR IT CANNOT BE REVERSED BY ANYONE EXCEPT THE SPELLCASTER WHO FIRST SETS IT INTO PLACE.

Orville Gold, genie historian of Feyland

I

I would have given up my wings to feel as peaceful as the scene outside. Gazing sadly through my mother's open window, I saw gold and silver rooftops strung across the hills. Red flowers higher than my shoulders waved in a wide field, and in the soft sand beyond the blossoms, young fairies and genies played a game of pot-o'-gold, their laughter ringing faintly across the morning air.

This was Galena, a place where most fairies would feel peaceful and safe. But I, Zaria, felt no peace. No peace, and not much safety either. Too much had happened in a few short days. Within weeks of turning fourteen, I had been hunted as a criminal throughout Feyland. My dearest friends were attacked. And my guardian was dead.

There was more too. More danger, more risks, and many secrets. Though I looked for the truth, large parts of it were still missing – and the more I searched, the less I seemed to find.

Sighing, I let my gaze fall from the window. On the desk in front of me lay a quill and an inkpot beside a piece of paper pilfered from Earth. Half the paper was covered in words – foolish words full of blotches, fear and hope.

I was writing to my lost mother, the mother I hadn't seen in more than five years. Dipping my quill, I continued.

Everyone said humans killed you on Earth, Mother. Everyone. And when you didn't return, I had to believe them. What else could I do? They convinced me you were dead — you and Father and my brother Jett. And because I believed it, I closed my heart to every memory of you. It was the only way I knew to keep going without you.

But two days ago, I heard a rumour that you might be alive. Can it be true? If so, you must surely be captives. Nothing else could keep you away for so long.

When the rumour reached me, I searched for you, casting a hundred spells to find you. But none showed me the smallest hint of where you might be.

I skipped over how I had screamed when all the enchantments failed, and how I kept my tears inside.

Even so, I keep hoping that I might see you again. And if you're alive, I believe I know who is holding you — that evil fairy, Lily Morganite. If she discovered you knew she was stealing magic from Feyland, she would stop at nothing to silence you.

I too have been her captive, and while under her control I endured great pain! I worry that if you have survived, she is making you suffer. As for me, I was wrapped in a cloak woven of troll magic, but only for one day. I don't want to imagine what she could have done to you over the course of five years.

Remembering that cloak, I felt again its weighted darkness squeezing my wings. Not even the touch of iron could hurt that way. The cloak had grown heavier with

3

every move I made. Even worse, it had snuffed out my magic as easily as a bucket of water quenches a flame.

But just when I was most helpless, just when Lily Morganite thought I could never free myself, something woke within me.

I turned the cloak to powder.

No one believed it could be done. All the members of the High Council of Feyland decided the cloak was a fraud, that trolls had never touched it. They said if it were real, no fairy could escape it.

But it was real. I felt its power, a force I hope never to feel again – the power of troll magic.

Mother, I wish you were here to tell me what sort of magic I called on to escape that cloak. Do you know what I did or how I did it? Whatever it was, I wish I could use that magic now, to find you and Father and Jett, and free you as I freed myself. Then you would be here beside me, alive and whole, instead of haunting me to write a message that may never reach you.

But the truth is, now at this moment I have only this flimsy paper and blotchy ink. And I don't know who I am.

Chapter Two

FEYLAND'S DURABLE SPELLS PROTECT THE FEY IN MANY WAYS, FROM ALLOWING SAFE TRAVEL TO AND FROM EARTH, TO MAINTAINING THE SCOPES THROUGH WHICH WE VIEW OUR HUMAN GODCHILDREN, TO SECURING THE GATEWAY OF GALENA, WHICH ALLOWS FEY CHILDREN TO GROW UP IN INNOCENCE AND SAFETY.

ALL DURABLE SPELLS MUST BE REFRESHED WITH MAGIC FROM TIME TO TIME, OR THEY WILL EVENTUALLY FAIL. THE FORCIER OF FEYLAND COLLECTS MAGIC TAXES AND USES THEM TO REFRESH THE DURABLE SPELLS AS NEEDED.

Orville Gold, genie historian of Feyland

Finishing my letter would have to wait. I put down my quill to go meet my friends.

We gathered beside the field of sonnia flowers. Meteor leaned on his elbows, his legs stretched out until his toes touched the flagstones of the little courtyard in front of my home. Across from me Leona sat gracefully, her lips red with sonnia juice, her silver eyes alert and eager for the news I had promised. Andalonus was plucking petals for her, his blue hair waving in the wind.

'I went to see Laz,' I began.

When Meteor heard Laz's name, he sat up and scowled until his white eyebrows met in a thick bar across the dark skin of his forehead. '*Laz?*' Meteor hated Laz, the lowlife genie who had tricked me and wrapped me in the troll cloak. 'Why would you go anywhere near that troggy smuggler?'

I did my best to return Meteor's scowl, but I'm not a scary sight at all. It's not only that I'm somewhat small, but I also have very plain colouring for a fairy. My skin and hair are both a pale shade of lavender, so my purple wings are the only part of me that stands out.

'What's the news?' Andalonus grinned at me, his coppery eyes gleaming. I smiled back. Who would not smile at Andalonus, the friend who had never doubted me – even when I was accused of murdering Beryl Danburite, my own guardian?

I shifted my wings. 'Laz said my family might be alive.'

Andalonus blinked. Leona squinted. Meteor frowned.

'And you believed him?' Meteor asked. 'A double-crossing liar?'

'He doesn't *always* lie.' I clutched my wand inside the pocket of my gown. 'And what if it's true? What if the councillors were lying when they told me humans killed my family? My parents travelled to Earth again and again! They must have known how to keep out of sight.'

Leona lifted her right hand, displaying livid burns across

6

her fingers. She unfurled her wings for a moment too, showing the charred line along the margin of one wing. 'Humans can be stupidly vengeful,' she said. 'Even more than fey folk.'

After almost getting killed on Earth, Leona didn't think any human could ever be trusted. And I had seen the one whose weapon burned her, so I knew how hasty and violent humans could be. But I didn't believe they were all alike. Some were not only kind but also fascinating.

I looked away from Leona's injuries. They reminded me that in Feyland, no healing spells exist. Her burns would soon become scars, scars she would wear for the rest of her life even if she lived to be two hundred and fifty.

Meteor's scowl was gone now, and he spoke softly. 'I'm sorry, Zaria. But your family has been gone for five years. How could they possibly still be alive?'

'Yes,' Leona added. 'If they were alive, they would have come back.'

Andalonus didn't say anything, but he nodded.

I looked from one to the other and took a long, quavery breath. Now more than ever, I needed my friends. I hoped they wouldn't decide I was just chasing coloured smoke – even if I probably was.

'Laz said Lily Morganite might have frozen my family in glacier cloth,' I said.

Chapter Three

SOME AMONG THE FEY BECOME OVERLY FOND OF EARTH. SUCH FAIRIES AND GENIES LOSE ALL PERSPECTIVE. THEY BEGIN TO BELIEVE THAT HUMANS ARE LOVABLE. THEY CONSIDER THE TREES OF EARTH TO BE MORE BEAUTIFUL THAN THE SHRUBS UPON TIRFEYNE. THEY WOULD RATHER SOAR THROUGH THE SKIES OF EARTH AND PLAY WITH HUMANS THAN ATTEND TO THEIR DUTIES IN FEYLAND. SUCH FEY FOLK ENDANGER US ALL. THEY ARE CALLED 'EARTH-STRUCK', AND THERE IS NO CURE FOR THEIR CONDITION.

Orville Gold, genie historian of Feyland

'Glacier cloth. That would be Lily's style,' Leona said bitterly.

Whenever I thought of my mother, my father, my brother, trapped and helpless, urgency seized me. I'd been told that anyone spellbound in glacier cloth would lose all sense of time. For them, whole years would disappear into one repeating moment of sudden cold. But the meaning of time was never lost on me. I had felt every moment of each day as five years passed without my family.

'Shh,' Meteor hissed. 'Did you hear that?'

The two genies rose up and looked around.

'Hear what?' I listened, but the air was quiet and perfectly calm.

Something seized my wrist. I twisted, but couldn't shake loose. I heard a scream and saw Leona struggling with another unseen foe. Then Meteor and Andalonus jerked as if strings had been tied to their joints and pulled tight.

Meteor ripped his hands free. He coiled his powerful body then let loose, striking out with fists and feet. Andalonus jabbed the air with his sharp elbows.

Grunts, yells, groans from our invisible attackers. How many were there?

Meteor fought his way towards me, grappling against unseen hands. Something yanked my wings, and I shrieked in pain. Meteor kicked whoever held me, freeing my wings and lifting me into the air.

Below us, deeper in the sonnia field, flowers waved like restless water. They parted, showing a horde of stocky creatures marching our way.

'Gnomes!' I shouted.

The gnomes wore brass helmets and breastplates, and they carried clubs of pounded iron. Iron!

Shouts erupted from the air beside us. 'Get the thieves! Stop them.'

But gnomes were unable to fly.

Drawing my wand, I poured magic into it. '*Chantmentum pellex!*' I cried.

My reversal spell made dozens of fairies and genies suddenly visible – a cloud of them, all unknown to me. They bunched around me and my friends, pushing and shoving and grabbing.

What were they doing in Galena?

I didn't have time to do another spell before five sets of hands began tearing at my wings, my hair, my gown. 'Give it back, thief!' an orange-winged fairy screeched in my face.

Meteor kicked furiously until he could draw his wand. '*Obliv trau!*' he yelled.

My attackers lost their grip: three genies and two fairies dropped to the ground asleep.

But instantly, another wave of strangers attacked.

As Meteor and I fought them off and tried to get closer to Leona, Andalonus rushed across the courtyard towards my door, beating at the air as he went. He pressed the latch and dived into the room beyond. An instant later he flew back outside clutching the poker from my hearth, whaling at the air, defending Leona, whose wings and hands were trapped. Her captors howled as the poker struck, and scrambled to get out of the way, fearing injury.

Leona's wings spread like a great silver fan, and her wand hand was free.

'*Obliv trau!*' she yelled, waving her wand in an arc.

Dozens more fey folk fell heavily to the ground, snoring.

'Quick!' I called. 'Get inside.'

Chapter Four

GNOMES, LIKE LEPRECHAUNS, ARE SHORTER AND STOUTER THAN FAIRIES AND GENIES. THEIR FAVOURITE MEAL IS A GRUEL MADE OF FINELY GROUND GRANITE OR LIMESTONE. THEY ARE NOT FOND OF COLOURS, SO THEIR GARMENTS ARE DRAB, AND THEIR SKIN AND HAIR ARE DULL.

GNOMES DWELL IN ALL PARTS OF THE WORLD OF TIRFEYNE, BUT THEY HAVE LIMITED MAGIC. THEY CANNOT FLY OR CAST SPELLS. THEY MAKE EXCELLENT GUARDS, BECAUSE A SPELL CAST DIRECTLY UPON A GNOME HAS NO EFFECT, AND GNOMES CAN HANDLE IRON WITHOUT INJURY.

THE FEAR FELT BY FAIRIES AND GENIES WHEN CONFRONTED WITH AN IRON WEAPON CANNOT BE DESCRIBED. FOR IRON NOT ONLY INTERFERES WITH MAGIC, IT ALSO BRINGS WEAKNESS AND FREEZING PAIN TO THOSE IT TOUCHES.

Orville Gold, genie historian of Feyland

I slammed the door and heard furious shouting from outside. A growling roar sounded like the air itself had been shaken by a band of trolls.

My friends and I waited, gasping and shaky.

Everything was suddenly quiet.

I flew to the window, the others right behind me. Peering out, I saw gnomes on the ground. Some lay stunned. Others staggered back and forth, dazed. Above them, a great crowd of fairies and genies buzzed angrily. The rest of our attackers had become visible.

And two wingspans away on the other side of the crystal pane, Lily Morganite appeared. Of course! She was the only one who could have led the attack. No one else had enough radia to cast spells of invisibility upon so many. And only Lily Morganite had ever pressed groups of gnomes into her personal service.

How was it possible that her face didn't show any of the evil inside her? Her pink skin was flawless, her saffron hair full of lustre and twined with rubies, her pearly eyes shining, white wings beating smoothly.

But this fairy was diabolical! When she had been Forcier of Feyland, she had collected magic tax from innocent fey folk and then kept it for herself instead of refreshing the durable spells – a crime my friends and I had uncovered only days earlier. And if Laz was right, Lily Morganite had trapped my parents and brother – all because they had guessed she was stealing magic from Feyland.

There wasn't any doubt that she had tried her best to divide me from my friends – especially Leona. She'd also done what she could to trick me into giving up my wand.

When her trickery didn't work, she had declared me a criminal and offered a reward for my capture. Laz delivered me to her, and then she deceived and enchanted every member of the High Council into believing I had killed Beryl, my guardian, when that terrible deed was done by Lily herself; I was sure of it. She even enchanted Leona to tell lies about me – Leona, who had been my friend since we were too young to fly!

And now Lily Morganite hovered outside my window in Galena, a place that should have been safe from her.

'Those fairies and genies don't belong in Galena any more than the gnomes,' Meteor said. 'The gateway must have fallen!'

As I stared, Lily picked up an iron club that lay beside a stunned gnome. She flinched as the iron touched her skin, but didn't drop it. Whirling it in an arc above her head, she threw it at the window.

My friends and I jumped back.

The club should have smashed the crystal panes. It should have come whistling into the room, striking anyone in its path. Iron always interfered with magic. But that club never struck the window. It bounced back towards Lily, who dodged. The club flew past her and hit the ground.

Leona let out a hissing breath. 'Oberon's Crown! A spell against *iron*?'

'You've enchanted your house?' Meteor asked in awe. 'What spell can keep out gnomes? And iron?'

'How did you do it, Zaree?' Leona asked.

I looked through the window. Lily was touching her throat with her wand. Her lips moved, and then I could hear her clearly. 'Open the door, Zaria,' she said, her voice amplified. 'I cannot get past your enchantments. But I have something to tell you.'

Chapter Five

ALL FAIRIES AND GENIES ARE BORN WITH RESERVES OF
MAGIC, WHICH ARE MEASURED IN UNITS CALLED *RADIA*. NO
MAGICAL ACTIVITY EXCEPT ORDINARY FLIGHT MAY BE DONE
WITHOUT SPENDING RADIA; VARIOUS SPELLS REQUIRE
GREATER OR LESSER AMOUNTS. FOR EXAMPLE, A SINGLE
JOURNEY TO EARTH AND BACK AGAIN USES HALF OF ONE
RADIA, WHEREAS OPENING OR CLOSING A *PORTAL* TO EARTH
REQUIRES 1000.

WHEN THEY TURN FOURTEEN, FAIRIES AND GENIES
RECEIVE A CRYSTAL WATCH THAT REGISTERS INBORN MAGIC
IN ADDITION TO TELLING TIME.

THE FACE OF THE WATCH IS DIVIDED INTO SIX
COLOURS, AND EACH COLOUR CONTAINS TEN DEGREES. IF
THE THIRD HAND OF THE WATCH POINTS TO THE FIRST
DEGREE OF RED, IT MEANS THE ONE WEARING THE WATCH
HAS TEN RADIA IN RESERVE. THE TENTH DEGREE OF RED
MEANS ONE HUNDRED RADIA. (NOWADAYS, 89 PER CENT OF
FAIRIES OR GENIES REGISTER AS RED, ALSO KNOWN AS
UNGIFTED.) THE ORANGE ZONE RANGES FROM ONE

15

HUNDRED RADIA TO ONE THOUSAND RADIA. (SIX PER CENT REGISTER AS ORANGE.) YELLOW GOES FROM ONE THOUSAND TO TEN THOUSAND. (FOUR PER CENT.) GREEN: TEN THOUSAND TO ONE HUNDRED THOUSAND. (LESS THAN ONE PER CENT.) BLUE: FROM ONE HUNDRED THOUSAND TO ONE MILLION. (ONE TENTH OF ONE PER CENT.) VIOLET: FROM ONE MILLION TO TEN MILLION RADIA. VIOLET IS SO RARE, SOME IN FEYLAND BEGAN TO BELIEVE THAT REGISTERING IN THIS COLOUR COULD HAPPEN ONLY IN THE REALM OF MYTH.

ALL MUST LEARN THAT A UNIT OF RADIA, ONCE USED, IS GONE FOR EVER.

Orville Gold, genie historian of Feyland

(M)eteor glided between me and the door. 'Don't open it,' he said.

'She can't come in,' I told him. 'If she could have, she would have.' Before he could argue, I darted past him and opened the door.

A cloying scent poured in, a scent I had learned to despise – the scent of lilies. Feeling sickened, I wished my wings wouldn't flutter. The magical barrier had proven itself, but still I trembled to see Lily Morganite without a wall or even a windowpane between us.

Her eyes looked like heated pearls. 'Your spells are well made, Zaria, beyond my skill to undo. For now.'

I hovered carefully behind the threshold. 'You said you had something to tell me.'

'A warning,' Lily said sweetly. 'You and Leona Bloodstone escaped me once, but only because luck favoured you. Do not rely on luck, Zaria.'

'Luck!' Leona shouted. 'I'll show you luck.' She was rushing forward, but Meteor and I caught her.

'Don't,' I cried. 'Stay back.'

Smiling, Lily watched as Leona controlled herself.

'You may be Violet fairies,' she continued, 'but my radia reserves are thousands of times greater than the two of you combined.' She flicked the air with her wand.

Thousands of times greater? We knew Lily had stolen a fortune from Feyland, but billions?

'How did you bring down the gateway?' Meteor fumed. 'And how dare you attack us in Galena?'

Lily's white wings carried her a little closer to the doorway. 'I did not attack; it was my followers.' She smiled gloatingly.

'When my father and the other councillors find out what you have done . . .' Meteor began.

But Lily laughed at him. 'The High Council is nothing more than a group of gibbering gremlins, young Zircon.' She ignored his frown, turning to me. 'I apologize for the attack, Zaria. It's just that my followers know you have wronged me; they wanted to make things right.'

I looked at the swarm of fey folk nodding their heads at her words, at the gnomes struggling to get up, and wondered what she had promised them. 'Wronged? You?'

As soon as I spoke, they all began yelling at once: 'Give it back, thief!' 'Vile robber!' 'Filthy cheat!'

Lily let their yells turn into roars before she held up her hand for silence.

'What lies have you told them?' I asked her when they had finally stopped hurling insults.

She shook her head at me, as if I were a child who should know perfectly well that I had committed a crime. 'They know you have stolen something of mine, Zaria. A bottle, holding the remains of a troll cloak you once wore.'

How easily she said it, as if that cloak had not almost cost me my life.

'You told them the bottle was *yours*?' I spluttered, and then realized my mistake.

I should not have admitted the bottle existed.

When my magic had risen up and turned the troll cloak into a heap of powder, Meteor advised me to save the powder. So I used a spell to gather it into a tall bottle made of indigo glass, the only container to hand. Now, that bottle stood on a shelf in my home, filled with fine powder, darkly shining. I feared its magic so much, I hadn't dared to open it. I could hardly even look at it, and when I did it seemed to stare back with a thousand eyes.

'It is mine by right.' Lily drew herself up, holding her wand like a sceptre.

By right! How did she even know I had it? No one knew, no one but my friends and me.

'Go away,' I said. 'The bottle isn't yours.'

'It is. But since you have it, I am willing to make an exchange,' she said. 'I offer to tell you your family's true story along with granting you a truce. For the bottle.'

I stared.

Meteor spoke up, his deep voice cutting. 'I don't believe you,' he told Lily.

'You are not the one who must believe, young genie.' She pointed at me. 'My offer expires in ten minutes, Zaria.'

I shut the door on her.

'Trolls and trogs!' Leona yelped.

Meteor paid no attention to Leona's rage. 'Where is the bottle of powder?' he whispered.

I showed my friends the shelf beside the potbelly stove. When I lifted the bottle, it felt heavier than it should. Though it wasn't any longer than my forearm and not quite as big around, it might as well have been the size of a troll.

'If it were anyone but Lily, I would turn this over here and now for the chance of finding my family,' I said.

'But it *is* Lily,' said Meteor.

'The powder must be very powerful.' Leona's silver eyes shone.

Andalonus pulled his ears. 'Maybe it multiplies magic.'

'Multiplies?' I shook my head.

Leona touched a wing to mine. 'He could be right, Zaree. How did you put such a strong spell on your house?'

'I've never opened the bottle,' I answered. 'I've avoided even touching it till now.'

'I doubt it increases magic,' Meteor said, rotating his shoulders the way he always did when he was puzzled and worried. 'But whatever it does, it must be something dire or Lily Morganite wouldn't be trying to take it.'

I shuddered. 'I won't let her have it,' I said, setting it down again.

Whatever happens, she must never get hold of it.

Chapter Six

LEVELS OF MAGIC GIVE THE CAPACITY TO PERFORM SPELLS FROM SIMPLE TO ADVANCED. FOR EXAMPLE, LEVEL 2 MAGIC ALLOWS THE CREATION OF COLOURED SMOKE OR OTHER SMALL ENCHANTMENTS. LEVEL 75 IS REQUIRED FOR THE CREATION OF PORTALS TO EARTH, WHEREAS TO *TRAVEL* THROUGH PORTALS, ONE MUST POSSESS AT LEAST LEVEL 5.

THERE ARE WIDE DIFFERENCES IN LEVELS. FOR EXAMPLE, MANY RED FAIRIES AND GENIES POSSESS ONLY LEVEL 4, WHEREAS A GIFTED FAIRY OR GENIE MAY BE AS HIGH AS LEVEL 100. IN RECENT TIMES, ONLY 10 IN EVERY 100,000 FAIRIES OR GENIES HAVE MAGIC TO LEVEL 20 OR HIGHER. INDEED, FEY MAGIC HAS BEEN DIMINISHING FOR CENTURIES.

LEVELS OF MAGIC ARE NOT THE SAME AS RADIA, FOR RADIA MEASURES *AMOUNTS* OF MAGIC.

Orville Gold, genie historian of Feyland

When I opened the door, the disgusting smell of lilies hit me in the nose. Outside, Lily hovered just above the ground.

'I won't bargain with you,' I told her firmly.

'And why not?'

'I don't trust you,' I answered.

'I have never promised you anything I did not deliver, Zaria.'

I focused on her followers. 'She will lead you to nothing but suffering,' I said. 'And death.'

A genie with granite-grey skin floated forward, sneering. 'We won't listen to a filthy thief, Zaria Tourmaline!'

Others began crowding near, yelling again, their faces twisted into angry frowns.

I closed the door, shutting them out, and hurried to pick up the indigo bottle.

In the hearth room, away from the lingering stench of lilies, I lit one of the fey globes on the wall with a touch. 'Sorry you've been dragged into this,' I said.

'We're your friends,' said Leona. 'Lily Morganite doesn't understand friendship, but we do.'

I smiled at her gratefully and moved to the nearest perch. 'Lily or no Lily, we have to find out what this *is*.' I hefted the bottle, then let it rest heavily in my lap.

'First, I want to know why the spell on your house was able to turn back iron – and gnomes.' Meteor found a place on a higher perch, his long legs swinging over the edge. 'What spell did you use?' he prodded.

Andalonus hovered just above the rug that lay in disarray

on the stone floor. 'Tell us, Zaria, or we'll be forced to listen to Meteor ask you over and over.'

Wrapping my wings around my shoulders, I admitted, 'I have a secret.'

None of them bothered to pretend they were surprised.

'Out with it.' Leona settled on the tattered cushions of the perch across from me, her silver wings folded.

I put both hands on the bottle's smooth glass. 'I've been casting spells with common words instead of using the ancient language.'

'What?' Meteor rocked forward so far he fell, and barely caught himself before hitting the floor. 'Only the ancient language can cast spells,' he said a little breathlessly. 'Every scroll in the Crown Library agrees.'

'But they're wrong,' I said.

'They can't be!'

'It started the day I met Lily,' I explained. 'She enchanted me in a web of sleep. I took flight, but I could feel her spell taking hold, and I've never been so desperate. We'd only just received our wands! I didn't know what to do, but I infused my wand and said, *Undo any spells on me.*'

'And?' Leona asked.

'Her spell was gone. At first I thought it had just expired on its own. But since then I've tried using common words many times. My spells always work.'

Leona was smiling now, an eager smile. 'We don't have to learn the ancient language?'

I nodded. 'We can make up spells.'

'That's impossible.' Meteor was not smiling. 'Otherwise, someone besides you would have discovered it.'

'I'm telling the truth.' I squeezed the neck of the bottle.

As usual, Leona wasted no time. She drew her wand, one of the most splendid in Feyland. Made of platinum twined with gold and silver filigree, it was tipped with bloodstone. 'Make coloured smoke.' She pointed into a corner.

Nothing changed. The fey light showed only empty shadows on the stone.

Then Meteor drew his wand, which was much less ornate. He jabbed its zircon tip at the kindling on the hearth. 'Light the fire.'

No spark moved. Meteor and Leona lifted their eyebrows at me while Andalonus watched from his perch near the window. As a Red genie with only Level 4 magic, Andalonus would never use his wand for guesswork. It was all so unfair: he didn't have enough magic to make a single journey to Earth even when he got older and it was allowed. I would gladly have given him the radia for trip after trip, but no amount of radia could change his inborn level.

When Meteor was revealed to be an impressive Level 50 Blue genie, he cared nothing for the opinions of the councillors of Feyland – including those of his father, Councillor Zircon – and refused to give up his friendship with Andalonus. The councillors openly despised Andalonus for his low magic, while treating me and Leona with a mix of flattery and resentment when we registered Violet. I began with full reserves of Violet; Leona with half full. And I am Level 100, while Leona is even higher: Level 200. We were told by our mentors that our friends would hate us for having such high-level magic, and that we should hold ourselves apart from them. We ignored that advice.

I set the bottle in the pillows of my perch, then drew out my wand. It was time to prove I had told the truth about using common words to create spells.

Leona snickered. 'Why don't you change your wand? You're a Violet fairy! That wand makes you look like a—' She stopped.

'Like a Red,' said Andalonus.

'I'm sorry,' Leona said. 'I didn't mean—'

'I agree with Leona.' Andalonus waggled his eyebrows at me. 'Your wand is pitiful.'

When my friends and I got our first chance to leave Galena for Oberon City, we had been so excited. The rule keeping us sheltered until our fourteenth birthdays seemed creaky and absurd. But when our wands were issued, they turned out to be human-made pieces of hard plastic. It was still hard to believe, yet true. We'd each received a simple stylus made on Earth! Before doling them out, the councillors had enhanced the plastic so that it could easily conduct magic.

Leona had been the first to transform her wand into a

thing of beauty. Meteor hadn't waited long to convert his to a more traditional form, either. But until now, I had resisted making any changes to my own.

Now I held it up. It *was* a rather pitiful object without gems of any kind. 'Change my wand to amethyst with a rose tourmaline tip,' I said. 'Make it a durable change.'

The stylus grew from matchstick width to as thick as my thumb. It went from black to sparkling purple. A rosy tip formed at the end.

Leona rushed to admire it. 'Perfect!'

Meteor and Andalonus crowded around too.

'How?' Meteor asked, looking at me sideways.

'Common words conduct magic just like a spell in the old language,' I said. 'But watch out – it still uses up radia.'

Meteor waved his wand again. 'Make coloured smoke,' he said. Nothing happened.

Leona twirled her wand. 'Light the fire.'

The hearth lay cold.

Chapter Seven

BEFORE A WAND MAY BE USED TO CAST A SPELL IT MUST
BE *INFUSED* WITH THE WAND-BEARER'S MAGIC. WHEN THE
BEARER INFUSES THE WAND, HE OR SHE SENDS MAGIC
THROUGH THE CORE OF THAT WAND, WHICH LIGHTS UP TO
REFLECT THE LEVEL THAT WILL BE APPLIED.

Orville Gold, genie historian of Feyland

Pulling aside the frayed curtain, I looked out. Dark streaks
of cloud ran across the sky and threw shadows on the
injured and angry crowd, but Lily Morganite was nowhere
to be seen. Where had she gone? I could almost feel her
prowling the borders of my protection spell, looking for any
chink I might have overlooked.

'Maybe common words don't work on small spells,'
I said.

'You try,' said Leona.

I infused my new wand to Level 2 and pointed at the
corner. 'Make coloured smoke.'

Clouds of misty red, blue and yellow swirled up from the
floor to mix in the air, making hazy purple, green and
orange.

I waved at the hearth. 'Light the fire.'

A spark ignited and the kindling burst into flame.

Andalonus clapped his hands. 'You cast all the enchantments on your house with common words?'

'All the ones for protection, yes.' I paused. 'I remember the exact words of that spell: *Only those who love me may enter this house as long as I'm alive; no one and nothing else may come into this house in any form.*'

Meteor's emerald eyes caught mine warmly. 'Our love for you is what lets us into your home?'

Andalonus leaped from his perch and swept me a bow. 'Clever one!'

Leona flew close to me. 'How much radia did it take?'

'Ten thousand.' A hundred times more than all Andalonus's stores. But after what had happened with Lily and Laz, I needed a refuge.

Leona nodded understanding, but she hadn't forgotten the indigo bottle. 'I still want to know if your magic has become stronger. Will you open your watch, Zaree, to see if your level is still one hundred?'

I flipped up the cover to my crystal watch. The face showed the six colours: red, orange, yellow, green, blue, violet. Two silver hands told me it was near nightfall: seven o'clock. The small golden radia hand pointed to just under the ninth mark of violet, meaning I had almost nine million radia left. In the centre of the watch, a luminous number said 100. 'Yes.' I held out my wrist.

Leona peered at my watch. 'You've used up more than a million radia?'

'A million!' Meteor jumped to grab my wrist and look for himself. 'I knew you were being careless, but . . . a million?'

I yanked my hand away. '*Careless?*'

'A *million?*' He looked down his genie nose at me.

'Destroying the cloak took *most* of it,' I said. 'I had no control over that!'

'No control?' he said. 'Why not?'

'My magic took over without me.'

'Then how did you infuse your wand?'

'I didn't. My wand was nothing better than a stick. The cloak had taken away my powers.'

The arrogance went out of Meteor's stance. 'Took away . . . ? You said it was *supposed* to take away your powers, but you—'

'The cloak's magic worked. At first. Until . . . something rose up and took over. I don't know what happened. I don't know what set off my magic.'

Meteor shook his head slowly. He folded himself onto the rug and gazed at me as if I were a puzzle he needed to solve.

Leona had been listening closely. 'You must be in possession of something else, Zaree; some other power that goes beyond levels of magic or colours of radia.'

I felt uneasy. 'How could I?'

'There was troll magic in that cloak,' Leona said.

Meteor looked up. 'Leona's right. Who can overcome the magic of trolls? None of the fey, not one, however high their level.' His eyes found mine. 'You're different from us.'

'Uncommon.' Leona touched her wing to mine.

Meteor didn't seem to hear her. '*You* can make spells with common words, Zaria. Only you.' He rubbed his knuckles over a threadbare patch of yellow in the rug. 'And you had the power to do it before you had that bottle.'

Chapter Eight

HUMAN ERRORS ABOUT FEY FOLK HAVE BECOME WIDE-
SPREAD. FOR EXAMPLE, HUMAN STORIES DEPICT NOT ONLY
FEMALE FAIRIES AND MALE GENIES, BUT ALSO MALE FAIRIES
AND FEMALE GENIES. THIS IS ABSURD.

FAIRIES ARE THE FEMALE OF THE SPECIES; GENIES ARE
THE MALE. FAIRIES HAVE WINGS, GENIES HAVE MAGIC FEET,
BUT BOTH CAN FLY WITH EQUAL SPEED. HUMANS APPEAR TO
BELIEVE THAT FAIRIES ARE TINY AND GENIES ARE
ENORMOUS. THIS IS NOT SO. ON AVERAGE, BOTH FAIRIES
AND GENIES ARE BETWEEN FIVE AND SIX FEET TALL WHEN
FULL GROWN, MUCH LIKE HUMANS.

FAIRY WINGS AND GENIE FEET ARE AUGMENTED BY
MAGIC; WITHOUT MAGIC, A FAIRY'S WINGS WOULD NOT BE
ENOUGH TO CARRY HER, AND A GENIE'S FEET WOULD NOT
BE ENOUGH TO CARRY HIM. BUT ALL FAIRIES AND GENIES
FLY, NO MATTER WHAT THEIR LEVEL OR COLOUR. THIS IS
THE ONE GREAT EQUALIZER: ALTHOUGH FLYING IS A
MAGICAL ACTIVITY, IT DOES NOT USE UP RADIA.

Orville Gold, genie historian of Feyland

I didn't like the way my friends were staring at me, as if they'd never seen me before. My wings fluttered uneasily. I wanted to say that Meteor didn't know what he was saying, that he was only guessing, that there must be others like me. But even more, I wanted everyone to forget what I had told them.

Leona broke the silence, saying, 'Whatever your unknown powers are, the bottle is what Lily's after, Zaria – not you.' She flapped a hand at the perch behind me. 'We need to test that powder so we'll know why she wants it.'

I was sure that Lily would take me too if she could. And I cringed at the thought of opening the indigo bottle.

'Test it on me,' Leona said. 'A small sprinkle.'

'No,' I told her, studying the bottle. 'What if it's harmful?'

'It's been here all along,' she said impatiently. 'It hasn't hurt us.'

'But it hasn't been open.' I turned to Meteor. 'Couldn't it be dangerous?'

He grunted. 'Of course it's dangerous. Lily Morganite wants it! And it started with trolls.' Meteor drifted up from the floor to lean against the mantel. 'Troll magic is too strong for us, which is why I don't understand how you melted one of their cloaks, Zaria. You're . . .'

'Pretty,' Andalonus said, kicking Meteor. 'You're trying to say she's pretty, aren't you?'

Meteor threw up his hands, smiling at me. 'Yes, that's what I was trying to say.'

Grinning, Leona floated forward to touch the bottle. Light from the fey globe glimmered on its surface and made its way into the glinting darkness beneath. 'The only way to test the powder is to use it on something.' She infused her wand to Level 2 and tossed her black hair over her shoulder. '*Colos smychen.*' A second cloud of coloured smoke filled the hearth, mingling with the last wisps of ordinary smoke left from my burned-out fire. 'Now,' she said. 'Add a sprinkle of powder, Zaree. See what happens.'

I shook my head, even more uneasy.

'Please?' It was rare for Leona to plead. 'We're safe in here,' she said. 'We can test just the teeniest bit. Then we'll know.'

I sighed. Meteor and Andalonus were both nodding slowly.

'All right, but I don't want it touching me,' I said. 'Me, or anyone.'

Reluctantly I infused my wand and tapped the bottle. 'Unseal.' I took out the stopper.

Meteor picked up a teacup from the table nearby. 'Put a little in here and then close the bottle again,' he suggested.

The smoky glass cup was one of the few items from Earth my parents had owned. Made by humans thousands of years ago, it had a lovely design, its handle shaped like flowing water. Before her disappearance, my mother had often used that cup to serve me sonnia tea. So had Beryl, my guardian, despite her hatred of anything that came from Earth.

While Meteor held the cup I tipped the bottle. The heavy powder poured like fine salt, its particles gleaming darkly. Replacing the cap, I tapped it with my wand and repeated a spell. 'Seal this bottle so none may open it or break it but me.' A seamless band appeared and fitted snugly around the cap.

I pushed the bottle down in the cushions of my perch. Taking the cup from Meteor, I drifted to the hearth where Leona's coloured smoke swirled and danced. There I shook the cup, scattering a smidgen of powder.

The colours vanished, and the smoke with them. It didn't take any time; the smoke didn't die down. It simply ceased to be.

Dread slid through me, and I began to shake. The cup still held a pinch of powder; before I could drop it, I set it down on the hearthstones and flew backward. Turning to my friends, I found them bunched together, trembling.

'I wanted you to sprinkle that on me,' Leona whispered.

'It doesn't strengthen magic,' said Meteor. 'It *kills* magic. Probably kills any magical being too.'

'It could have killed *me*.' Leona's silver eyes had turned grey with fright. 'Never listen to me again, Zaree.'

Chapter Nine

It is unfortunate that fairies and genies born with high-level magic and large reserves of radia are not also born with wisdom. For when powerful fairies and genies practise magic for selfish purposes, all of Feyland suffers. Indeed, wicked fairies and genies have created mischief and misery for other fey folk on many occasions. The worst such case was that of Brone Granite, the evil genie who nearly succeeded in overthrowing King Oberon the Seventh.

Orville Gold, genie historian of Feyland

'Lily wants the powder because it's a weapon.' Leona's eyes had changed back to silver. 'It's the answer to our problems.'

'No,' I said. 'It's not an answer to anything.'

'It makes us Lily's equal. We can use it to defeat her.' Leona made a sprinkling motion, as if she held a cupful. 'We'll put some on her head.' She turned to Meteor. 'Would it kill her, or just get rid of her magic?'

Meteor's eyebrows went up. 'I don't *know* what it would do.'

'You said—'

'I *guessed*,' Meteor broke in. 'Remember, Lily knows much more about magic than any of us. And besides—'

'We have to get rid of it!' I cried. 'It's too dangerous to keep.'

'Too dangerous to lose,' Leona shot back.

Gazing past her at the mantelpiece, I noticed my family clock had stopped working. The engraved silver was still beautiful, but the hands were unmoving, the small golden pendulum silent and still.

My unease was growing.

'Leona—' I stopped as I caught a whiff of nauseating scent. Sweet, sticky and thick, it coiled around me.

Lilies.

I felt strangled. Something had gone wrong. When I closed the door on Lily, that smell had lingered near the doorway. But it shouldn't be getting stronger.

I whirled round, and screamed at what I saw. Lily Morganite hovered above the hearthstones.

Lily Morganite was *inside* my home.

Scrambling away from her, I spread my wings, hovering in front of the perch that held the indigo bottle. Meteor was on my left, Andalonus and Leona on my right. As one, we held up our wands.

Lily bent quickly to pick up the cup I'd left next to the ashes. She handled it as if it were the most precious and dangerous thing in the world, and trilled her gloating laugh.

'How predictable, Zaria. You could not leave well enough alone.'

'How did you get in?' I panted.

Lily raised the cup. 'This powder opened the way. It will be your doom, Zaria – unless, of course, you give the rest of it to me. I know how to dispose of it.' Light moved in the core of her wand, and she tapped the side of the cup. '*Crea viditas.*' A glass lid appeared, fitting tightly over the rim. I heard Meteor gasp, startled by her magic. Creating anything from nothing used up radia rapidly, but apparently she didn't care.

Lily slipped the cup into a pocket of her gown and opened her hand. 'Give me the bottle, Zaria, and I will tell you what you long to know.'

I refused to look at the perch behind me, but I couldn't stop my wings from fluttering. What if the neck of the bottle were visible? I remembered pushing it into the cushions, but I hadn't taken care to cover it completely.

'*You* do not understand ancient magic.' Lily floated forward an inch and stopped. Her wings were definitely quivering. Stranger still, her wand was still lit as if she were in the middle of doing a spell. '*I* have studied it for a hundred years.'

A hundred years. So, she was a powerful fairy in her prime. I had wondered about her age; it had been impossible to guess.

'Then tell us what you know.' I heard a tinge of hope in Meteor's voice.

'I will tell you this much,' she said harshly. 'The hole in your protections is permanent, Zaria. The effects of the powder can never be undone.' She patted her gown. 'And the small amount I have is worth more to me than the entire bottle is worth to you.'

'What will you do with it?' Meteor asked.

She tilted her head. 'This is your last chance to bargain, Zaria.' Her voice was menacing, but her wings beat so unsteadily I expected her to lose her balance and fall into the ashes on the hearth.

'No,' I answered.

'Then I will leave you,' she said coldly. 'For now.'

Chapter Ten

THE ROLE OF SCHOLAR IS RARELY GIVEN FULL APPRE-
CIATION. FORTUNATELY TRUE SCHOLARS FIND GREAT
SOLACE IN SEEKING KNOWLEDGE FOR ITS OWN SAKE.

Orville Gold, genie historian of Feyland

The second Lily vanished, I dug the indigo bottle out of
the cushions of my perch. Flying up to the first storey
too fast, I almost crashed against the door to my mother's
room before I could open it. My friends were right behind
me, and we all hurried inside. Meteor slammed the
door.

I placed the bottle on a shelf. There it rested quietly, but
its peril seemed to shout.

'I destroyed the protections on my own hearth with that
powder!' Trying to calm myself, I stared at the picture on
the wall, the painting of a forest of trees on Earth. But
though the sight normally soothed me, just then it didn't
help in the least.

'She couldn't come any closer,' Andalonus said.

'What?' Leona asked.

'Lily. She couldn't come all the way into the room. She
wanted to. Anyone could see she hates us worse than a trog

hates a bath. But she stayed near the spot where the powder was sprinkled.'

'Right, she did,' Meteor said, nodding. 'And her wings were quivering. She tried to hide it, but she couldn't.'

'I saw that too,' I agreed.

'She was careful not to touch the ashes where you threw the powder,' Meteor said.

'You think it's still active?' I asked, shivering. 'What if Lily's right about the effects being permanent?'

Andalonus bobbed nervously. 'Lily would say anything.'

I stared at the tiles in the floor – tiles formed into a spiral pattern in every shade of blue and green from pale turquoise to deep indigo, from light jade to the dark green of raw copper. 'She *knew* she'd find an opening,' I said. 'She was just waiting for us to test the powder.' My home had been a protected refuge for only a few days. Now it had danger at its heart.

'Should we test the house?' Meteor asked. 'Find out whether the hole in your spell closed up again?'

I shook my head. 'How? Have a party and invite fairies who hate me? See if they can get in?'

I looked around my mother's room, her lovely, abandoned room, the room she hadn't seen for five years. Sharp arrows of sadness took aim at me. What would Lily Morganite do next?

'We could protect ourselves,' Leona said. 'Each of us

could take some of the powder and carry it with us. Sealed, so it can't hurt us.'

'No,' I said.

'We'd use it only if needed.'

'I won't give you something that could kill your magic.'

Leona lifted her injured hand. 'It's all we have against Lily!' My fairy friend looked ready for battle, her silver eyes glinting like blades.

'If any of it touched you, you could end up like me.' Andalonus pointed at himself. 'Ungifted. A dire fate, Leona.'

Leona smiled at him. 'Ungifted or not, you're still the best of genies.' She lifted her chin. 'Besides, Lily could be lying about the powder. How could it last for ever?'

'She could be,' Meteor said. 'But we need to research it.'

I nodded eagerly. If anyone could learn about the powder, it was Meteor Zircon, a born scholar. The first place he wanted to go when we were allowed to visit Oberon City was the Crown Library, where he sought out ancient tomes. I would rather join a tribe of trolls, but Meteor enjoyed reading even the dustiest pages.

'Maybe there's a mention of it in one of the old texts. I'll go to the Crown Library,' he offered. 'If it's still standing.'

'Still standing?' I cried.

Meteor was much too solemn. 'We don't know what Lily plans,' he said. 'But why did she steal all that magic? And what did she want with Zaria's powder? She's up to

41

something.' He shook his head. 'And if I were an evil fairy, the Crown Library is the first thing I'd destroy. It's full of knowledge – knowledge that might defeat her.'

Andalonus scrunched up his forehead. 'If *you* were an evil fairy, you would make us study *with* you.'

Chapter Eleven

FIFTY YEARS AGO, THE LEPRECHAUN EDICT WAS PROCLAIMED BY THE HIGH COUNCIL OF FEYLAND. IT PROHIBITS LEPRECHAUNS FROM EVER TRAVELLING TO EARTH. THE EDICT WAS ENACTED TO ADDRESS TWO PROBLEMS. FIRSTLY, LEPRECHAUNS COULD NOT BE PERSUADED TO STOP TEASING HUMANS. THEY WOULD PUT POTS OF FEY GOLD IN PLAIN SIGHT, THEN CAUSE THEM TO VANISH. HUMANS HAVE NO SENSE OF HUMOUR WHEN IT COMES TO GOLD: WHEN THEY REALIZE THEY HAVE BEEN TRICKED, SOME OF THEM DEVELOP DANGEROUS GRUDGES. SECONDLY, LEPRECHAUNS BEGAN SMUGGLING HUMAN BEVERAGES INTO FEYLAND, WITH DISASTROUS RESULTS.

TO FACILITATE THE EDICT, ALL LEPRECHAUNS WERE SENT TO THE IRON LANDS, WHERE THEY LIVE IN WHAT IS KNOWN AS THE LEPRECHAUN COLONY. THE GROUND THERE IS MADE OF IRON ORE. NO MAGIC IS POSSIBLE, INCLUDING PORTALS TO EARTH. ANY ENCHANTMENTS BECOME NULL AND VOID FOR THE DURATION OF A STAY IN THE IRON LANDS.

Orville Gold, genie historian of Feyland

43

The crowd outside was gone, even the injured. Not so much as a single gnome remained.

I found it odd that none of my neighbours came by to ask after me. My father had built this home in a secluded spot but it wasn't secluded enough to be truly isolated. Had Lily used more radia to throw forgetting spells on those who might have seen the attack? It seemed unlikely, but why else would everyone in Galena ignore what had happened?

I shrugged off my gloom as my friends and I made plans. While Meteor went to the Crown Library, Leona and Andalonus were going to explore Oberon City to see what was happening there. We agreed to meet the following evening in my mother's room.

Alone, I picked up the indigo bottle. The glass felt bland and cool, as if it held nothing more than sand. Appearances could be so deceiving. Wasn't that often shown in the stories humans told their children? The frog is really a prince. The beauty has a cruel heart. The crippled old woman asks for shelter and, when turned away, proves to be a powerful fairy with a curse on her lips.

'We're going on a journey,' I told the bottle, and wrapped it in a yellow scarf that had belonged to my mother. I too would research the powder, but my way would be different to Meteor's.

I took the plainest woven bag I could find – black with

a grey border. Placing the bottle inside it, I stuffed more scarves around it before I slung the long strap around my neck. Then I created a spell of disguise to change my colouring. I turned myself from a lavender fairy with purple eyes and wings into a green-skinned fairy with black eyes and hair, and grey wings. The spell would last till I reversed it. It cost me twenty-five radia.

I brought to mind a certain sleazy café. 'Transport me to the Ugly Mug,' I said.

In less than an instant, I arrived. The Ugly Mug looked the same as it had the last time I'd been there only a few days before. Rough gravel paved the ground around a building made of unmatched stones and sloppy mortar. The copper door was so tarnished that not a bit of it shone, not even the grimy knob.

Meteor would be angry if he knew I was here. The owner of the place was none other than Banburus Lazuli – known as Laz – who had trussed me inside the troll cloak and turned me over to Lily Morganite for a reward of 50,000 radia.

Laz didn't have much in his favour, but he did have two things. One, he had never received that reward. Lily double-crossed him, which made him hate her. And two, he had turned the Ugly Mug into a place where endless streams of secrets trickled into his long ears. As I had tried to convince Meteor, Laz *knew* things, and I wanted answers.

I moved the bag holding the indigo bottle to my hand.

Clutching it firmly, I opened the café door. Sagging hinges squealed. Inside, the place was dimly lit by wax candles burning in globes half covered in soot. No fey lights here, but the aroma was heady – a mix of the forbidden flavours of cocoa and coffee from Earth.

I made my way past tables crammed with customers, ignoring brazen genies asking me to share their mugs of cocoa. Laz was in the back playing cards with four genies and a gnarled leprechaun who wore a crumpled old cap with a pitiful red feather. When I came close to their table, Laz looked up. His eyes narrowed for an instant. Then he went back to the game.

I wondered what the leprechaun was using to back up his bets. It couldn't be radia. Unlike fairies and genies, leprechauns could not transfer their magic. If they could, Lily Morganite would never have left them in the Iron Lands. She would have mined them like rubies.

But if not radia, then what could Laz be hoping to win?

He showed all his blue teeth in a smile, and made his bet: 'Two cases of that new stuff you're drinking. I call it Le-MoCo – the finest blend of cocoa and coffee from the far-flung reaches of Earth. And may I remind you, there's also a case of Terrabon candies to go with it.'

The four genies scowled at their cards. One, brown-faced with limp yellow hair, spoke up. 'Why is it, Laz, that every time the pot's this rich, you always seem to win?'

Laz picked up his own mug and took a long swallow.

'Makes up for all the dangerous trips I take to Earth to get confections for you ungrateful trogs.'

The genies shook their heads and tossed their cards. The brown-faced fellow muttered, 'Last time I called a bet like that, I spent a month washing the floors of this filthy den.'

Laz nodded and shrugged, then rapped the table with a fist. 'Meechem, do you call?'

The leprechaun cleared his throat noisily. 'Got nothing left.'

'Well,' Laz told him, 'if you like the look of your cards and you want to call my bet, I would accept that cap you're wearing.'

So. The cap was what Laz wanted.

Meechem shook his head. 'Don't want to part with my cap. Been in my family fifty generations. Special, it is.'

'Mud in your eye.' Laz pushed a large mug towards the leprechaun. 'Have another cocoa.'

Meechem took a hearty sip. His cap sure didn't look like much.

'Call?' Laz asked again, voice patient, smiling as if he and Meechem were great friends.

Sighing, Meechem took off his cap and laid it on the table. 'Call.'

Laz spread his cards face up.

I knew nothing about what made a winning hand, knew nothing of cards beyond Beryl's warnings against them. She always said I should beware; that card games, like other vices imported from Earth, had ruined many a genie and more than a few fairies.

They would not ruin Laz, at least not tonight. When Meechem saw Laz's cards, the corners of his mouth drew down so far I thought his lips would slide down his shaggy white beard into his neck.

Laz reached for the cap and crammed it over his stringy grey-blue hair. Somehow, it fitted him, though his head was noticeably bigger than Meechem's. 'Come back again,' he said. 'You're always welcome.'

He stood, and so did the other genies, but Meechem laid his head down on his arms. As Laz passed him, he patted his shoulder.

'Something I can help you with?' he asked as I hovered in front of him.

'I'd like a word.'

'Just one?'

'Privately.'

He shrugged, grabbing his mug from the edge of the table. 'Follow me.'

As I hurried after him, everyone we passed had something to say.

'I thought you only robbed human cradles!' hooted a snaggle-toothed genie.

A fairy with red eyes lifted her mug. 'Stolen beans!' she cackled.

'Fly while you can, little fairy,' advised a leprechaun.

Laz led me out of the door and round the corner of the café to a bare patch of gravel – the same place we'd talked the last time we met. Now it was dark. Above, a few stars tried to shine through the overcast night. They didn't cast enough light to see another building a little way off, even more rundown than the Ugly Mug. But I knew it was there, just as I knew that fifty wingspans back, the border wall of the Iron Lands snaked along the ground.

Laz leaned against the café wall and raised his mug to me. I recognized the scent of coffee. 'Terrible disguise,' he said, and took a drink.

'What do you mean?'

'I mean, Zaria Tourmaline, that it's a rotten disguise, and I hope you haven't been trying to hide from anyone who matters.'

'But––' I looked at his cynical smile. 'How did you know?'

'Did you forget we've met before? Next time, you might consider changing your features along with your skin colour.'

I pressed my lips together.

'Don't look so woeful. I've done you a favour letting you know your disguise isn't worth a single radia, let alone twenty-five.'

I frowned as he chuckled.

'What brings you?' Laz tipped his head back and poured the dregs of his coffee down his throat. 'Flattered as I am to get a visit from you, Zaria, I assume you didn't come here for my company.'

Trying to look casual, I put my hand in the pocket of my gown to touch my wand. 'I have questions.'

Laz rubbed his empty mug against his cheek and sighed. 'I'll give you the first answer for free, Zaria. *I don't know where your family is.* If I did, I would try to take you for every last radia you've got.' He let the mug hang from one finger. It swayed back and forth. 'As to any other question you may have, I'll give you each answer for two hundred radia.'

What a trog he was. 'Too steep,' I said. '*Fifty* radia.'

A glint of greed showed in his eyes. 'Maybe this once, then. Ask away.'

Chapter Twelve

THERE IS ONE METHOD FOR FEY FOLK TO GAIN MORE RADIA. THIS IS DONE BY TAKING A TRANSFER FROM SOMEONE ELSE'S WAND. DEPENDING UPON HOW MUCH RADIA IS AVAILABLE, IT IS POSSIBLE TO TRANSFER ANY AMOUNT FROM ONE WAND TIP TO ANOTHER.

TRANSFERS OF RADIA FROM WAND TO WAND CAN ONLY BE DONE VOLUNTARILY. NOT EVEN A COMPULSION SPELL CAN FORCE ANYONE TO TRANSFER THEIR MAGIC WITHOUT CONSENT.

FAIRIES AND GENIES WHOSE LIVES ARE DRAWING TO A CLOSE MAY DECIDE TO TRANSFER THE REMAINDER OF THEIR RADIA RESERVES TO ANOTHER. IF THIS IS NOT DONE, THE AMOUNT OF RADIA LEFT UNUSED AT THE TIME OF DEATH DISAPPEARS FOR EVER.

Orville Gold, genie historian of Feyland

I almost burst out with my most urgent question for Laz, but then thought of something else. 'I want an agreement. I get the same rate in the future. Any question for fifty radia, anytime I want. And you swear on your wand to tell no one what we talk about.'

If he swore on his wand and broke his word, the wand would turn against him. Not even Laz would take that lightly.

The genie's eyes moved back and forth. 'All right,' he said slowly. 'But it can't be an open-ended agreement. For three days, I will answer any of your questions for fifty. And I swear on my wand to tell no one what gets said.'

Knowing my luck with Laz, on the fourth day I would have an important question only he could answer. I should bargain for more, but I was tired and I doubted he'd budge. 'Done,' I said.

He yanked his cap to a more jaunty angle. 'First question?'

'Tell me what you know about the troll cloak you used to capture me.'

He laughed a snorting chuckle. 'It seems I was deceived about that cloak, since you made it disappear.'

'What was it supposed to do?' I didn't like wasting a question on something I already knew, but I wanted to hear him say it again.

Laz scratched his shoulder. 'It was supposed to make it impossible for you to use magic. And create pain that would get worse with any move you made.'

'You didn't care about my suffering?'

'That's your third question, Zaria. And it seemed like a good idea at the time.'

As anger flared along my wings, I drew my wand. Laz eyed it, but didn't seem as nervous as he should have been.

'Changed your wand, I see,' he said.

There was a long pause, and then I smiled at him. I'm sure anyone watching would have called it a grim smile – it felt grim on my face. 'What magic is in the cap you wear on your head?'

Laz looked at me as if I had just cheated in a card game. 'No enchantment cast by anyone in Feyland can affect me while I wear it.'

I returned his look. 'So even Lily Morganite can't get to you again?'

'Correct.' He blew out a breath. 'That's *five* questions, asked and answered. Pay up now or our bargain is off. Two hundred and fifty radia.'

Trolls and pixies! Although it was I who had blurted out two questions I didn't intend to ask, I felt as if Laz had tricked me.

I lifted my wand and infused it. He drew his own, which was brass with a lapis tip. Touching mine to his, my anger surged as I felt the magic of two hundred and fifty radia leave me and pass to Laz.

'More questions,' I told him. 'Have you seen Lily Morganite since the last time I was here?' *Question one.*

He grinned, satisfied with an easy answer. 'No.'

'If the troll cloak had a residue,' I said, 'what sort of magic would be in it?'

53

'Residue?' Laz sounded alarmed. 'Residue,' he repeated. 'What do you mean? You made the cloak disappear.'

'But if there *had* been a residue—'

He dropped his mug; it cracked and broke in pieces. Pressing both hands against the wall behind him, Laz stared at me. 'What have you done?' he whispered.

'Me!'

'You.'

'What have *I* done?' I flew at him, stopping just short of ramming into him. 'What did *you* do? Sold me out, as if I were a case of cocoa.'

He was shaking his head and running his hands through his stringy hair. 'Who has this . . . residue?' His voice was so hollow I wanted to whack his head to see if there was anything left inside. 'Tell me Lily Morganite does not have it.'

'She doesn't.'

He seemed to recover a little – he stopped propping himself against the wall.

'I kept it,' I said, glad I wasn't bound to tell him everything. If I revealed that Lily had a few grains, he might quit breathing right in front of me. 'Tell me what it does and how I can get rid of it.' I knew it was two questions, but maybe he wouldn't notice.

'The *aevum derk*,' he said, pitching his voice very low. 'I never believed . . .'

'What did you call it?'

'Aevum derk. The death of magic. It's said that a pinch

54

can destroy any spell or enchantment, no matter who or what it comes from.' Laz, the most blasé of genies, shivered like a bug in a storm. 'How much do you have?'

'A tall bottle. It's almost full.'

'A bottle. How did you know you should store it in glass? How did you know that only glass can contain aevum derk?'

I shuddered. I hadn't known. In truth, it was only luck that had led me to gather the aevum derk into a glass bottle. I shuddered again, realizing that I could easily have destroyed myself, my friends, and the entire High Council of Feyland. They had all been close by at the time.

But I wasn't going to tell Laz about that.

'Who else knows you've got it?' he asked.

I shut my lips. No reason to tell him about my friends.

'Does the Morganite know?'

I must have winced, because Laz started cursing softly at the sky, a long string of words, most of which I'd never heard. When he turned his attention back to me, he was brief. 'You're doomed. She'll stop at nothing to find you and take the aevum derk.' His head swivelled from side to side.

'She won't be looking for me *here*,' I said. 'Your café is probably the one place in Feyland she would never believe I'd go. You wrapped me in the cloak, remember? That's how it all began, Laz.' I gripped my wand a little tighter. 'Tell me more about the powder. How long do its effects last?'

He yanked on a lock of his lank hair. 'For ever.'

Chapter Thirteen

A *TROG* IS A MYTHICAL CREATURE. IF TROGS EVER EXISTED, THEY DIED OUT LONG AGO. AND YET, IGNORANT FEY FOLK PERSIST IN BELIEVING THAT TROGS CAN BE FOUND LIVING DEEP WITHIN TROLL COUNTRY.

A TROG'S HEAD IS SAID TO RESEMBLE THAT OF AN EARTH TOAD, EXCEPT THAT A TROG'S EARS ARE VERY LARGE, ALLOWING THEM TO HEAR WHISPERS FROM A LONG DISTANCE. TROGS ARE SAID TO WALK UPRIGHT, CANNOT FLY, AND EXUDE A PUTRID ODOUR THAT EVEN REPEATED BATHING CAN NEVER ERADICATE.

ACCORDING TO LEGEND, TROGS HAVE SUCH VILE DISPOSITIONS, THEY ARE UNABLE TO FORM COMMUNITIES BUT LIVE TO ANNOY EACH OTHER AND ANY OTHER SPECIES CROSSING THEIR PATHS.

Orville Gold, genie historian of Feyland

'For ever!' Had Lily told us the truth? 'Do you mean it can be used over and over?' I asked Laz.

'No. Once thrown against magic, it disappears. But its effects linger in the place where it's been used. *Ad eternum.*'

For ever and always.

'You're lying.'

'I wouldn't lie about this.'

I hovered at the right height to look the tall genie in the eye. 'How do you know?' *How many questions have I asked?*

He jerked his head towards the border wall. 'Magic isn't possible in the Iron Lands. Do you think every inch of those lands are covered with iron dust?'

Yes, I did. That's what they'd taught us in school.

'Why do you think no one living there can do magic?' he went on.

I gulped. 'But—'

'That's right, my fine fairy. An entire region of Feyland where magic is dead.'

Magic dead? An entire region of Feyland? The tote bag in my hand felt even heavier.

'But didn't you say you'd been there many times?' I asked. 'And *you* can still do magic.'

Laz flapped a hand dismissively. 'Yes, I've been there, and yes, I can still do magic – when I return. But the aevum derk was cast millennia ago, so the powder never landed on me. Its effects endure upon the land.'

'No one can overcome it, ever?' I dropped to the ground very ungracefully; I had to give my wings relief from the full weight of the indigo bottle.

He rubbed his chin. 'It would take a thousand units of radia at Level One Hundred to overcome the effects of one grain of aevum derk. No one has that kind of magic to spare.'

I thought of Lily hovering on my hearth, her wings quivering under an unknown strain. She was a Level 100 fairy! And she had used magic to transport in, and magic to stay, and magic to transport out. That's why her wand stayed lit! She must have used up many thousand units of stolen radia just to get a pinch of aevum derk.

What had she said before she left? *The small amount I have is worth more to me than the entire bottle is worth to you.* She must have plans for it. Where would she take it, and how would she use it?

'Where is the powder?' Laz asked.

I held his gaze and didn't look down, but I was afraid the scarves didn't really cover the bottle in the bag I carried. 'I won't tell you,' I said. 'But if you let me know how to get rid of it, I will.'

He gave his coughing laugh. 'Get rid of it? You can't. The only way to make it disappear is to throw it against magic. That's how it gets used up.' I heard whooping shouts from inside the café but Laz ignored the noise and kept talking. 'To offset an entire bottle of aevum derk, you'd have to cast it against spells worth billions of radia.'

Billions! Oberon's Crown! I had to find a way to hide the aevum derk, hide it somewhere no one could disturb it – *ad eternum*. For ever and always.

Both Laz and I were quiet. He was slumped against the

wall, and I couldn't find the strength to leave the ground; my wings felt like wilted petals.

Then Laz surprised me by straightening up and grinning wickedly. 'Wait a hot chocolate minute.' He leaned forward with his face so close to mine I could see every one of his blue teeth. 'You're not doomed, Zaria. You can defeat the Morganite,' he whispered.

I frowned. 'Defeat her?'

Laz lifted his nose. 'You have aevum derk! The mightiest weapon ever made in this world. Shake it on Lily and her wand. Instant victory.'

Leona had urged me to do the same. Now, I imagined how it would feel to take away Lily's magic – all of it. I'd never have to wonder what she might be plotting and which of my friends she might harm; never have to worry how much of Feyland she might destroy.

Laz tapped my shoulder, bringing me back to the night, the stars, the moment. Booming music was rattling the café, where leprechauns and genies belted out a song so loudly I could hear the words: '. . . *running the cocoa, leaping the laws . . .*'

'You see?' Laz said. 'Use the aevum derk against Lily. Simple solution.'

In some ways, yes, it would be. It would take away the threat of Lily Morganite. But what about the problem of hiding the aevum derk so no one else could use it either? And what about all of Lily's stolen radia?

'What's wrong?' asked Laz. 'Afraid? Mab's marshmallows, Zaria! You can't win big without a little risk.'

I glared at him thoughtfully. 'If I destroyed Lily's magic, billions of radia would be lost for ever.'

'No doubt.' The genie tugged the brim of his leprechaun cap.

'Would it kill her?'

'Might.'

But if she dies, she can't tell me about my family.

'We could never fix the durable spells,' I said.

Laz sneered. 'Always the good little fairy. Why would the durable spells concern *you*? The less magic there is in Feyland, the more powerful *you* will be.' He bowed to me with a false flourish. 'You're still Violet, aren't you?'

'Powerful in a dying land?' I cried. 'What good is that?'

'Good.' Laz spat the word as if it were a bitter sprig of bannerite. 'Don't be a fool. Will you or won't you do what must be done?'

Rotten smuggler! He had no right to push me. None. How I'd love to fly away this minute and never see him again. But I needed one more answer. 'I don't know,' I said. 'But I have one last question.'

He shrugged. 'The more you ask, the richer I get.'

'How is the aevum derk made?'

The genie looked at me sourly. 'That's my question for *you*. How did you do it, Zaria? How did you transform troll magic?' His murky eyes were at half mast as usual. Then they popped wide. 'Hobs and hooligans! Why didn't I see it before?'

'See what?' I demanded.

'You're one of the Feynere,' he whispered.

'The what?'

'The Feynere.' He peered at me. 'Your kind died out so long ago it's a wonder there's a word for you. And yet, here you are.' He swept me a shaky bow. 'Banburus Lazuli, at your service.'

'What do you mean?'

'A long, long time ago, Zaria,' he rasped, 'there were fey folk with astounding powers. Each one had Violet reserves of radia and Level One Hundred magic. They could protect themselves with unknown spells. And they had magic that could do unexpected things.' He grinned an eerie, twisted grin. 'You're one of them. A Feynere.'

'I don't believe you. How could I be one of them when I've never heard a single word about them?'

More grinning. 'I know how I missed it. A Feynere should be magnificent! Not a smallish fairy with rather plain colouring. No disrespect intended.'

Laz was looking at me as if he knew my darkest secrets. I had to get away from him.

'I need to be going,' I said, realizing I had lost count of the questions I'd asked. 'How much do I owe?'

His eyeballs snicked back and forth as he began ticking on his fingers. 'One,' he said, and then murmured to himself.

'Two.' More murmurs. 'Three. Four.' Laz grinned and went on counting. 'Fifteen questions. Seven hundred and fifty radia will cover it.'

'What!'

He drew his wand again. 'When it comes to bargains such as this, I never cheat.'

I couldn't prove he was overcharging. And I couldn't wait to leave. So even though I hated to pay him, I did, while the drums pounded and the fiddles whined, and someone bellowed another verse to the same song: '. . . *human folk, earthen ware, mud in your eye . . .*'

Before I left, I gave Laz what I hoped was a sinister stare. 'You swore to tell no one,' I said. 'And that means no one, for any price.'

He put up his hands as if the thought of selling me out had never crossed his greedy mind. 'Of course.'

'If you betray me again, I'll visit you when you least expect it. I'll sprinkle that cap with aevum derk; I'll sprinkle your head too.'

He smiled. 'I want only to serve you, Zaria Tourmaline.'

I didn't say farewell. Slinging the bag around my neck, I shot into the dark sky.

Chapter Fourteen

ONCE UPON A TIME, GODMOTHERS AND GODFATHERS WOULD INTERVENE IF THEY PERCEIVED THEIR GOD-CHILDREN IN TROUBLE, BUT THIS HAS BECOME RATHER RARE. THE MAJORITY OF GODMOTHERS AND GODFATHERS BEING RED, THE CAPACITY TO GIVE ASSSISTANCE TO HUMANS HAS DECLINED. HOWEVER, MOST FAIRIES AND GENIES STILL LOOK IN UPON THEIR GODCHILDREN BY USING THE FEY SCOPES. THE SCHEDULE OF VIEWING BOOTHS REMAINS BUSY, DAY AND NIGHT.

FEY SCOPES THAT VIEW EARTH ARE A GLORIOUS CREATION OF THE ANCIENTS. A SCOPE CAN TRACE THE MOVEMENTS OF ANY PERSONAGE — INCLUDING NOT ONLY HUMANS, BUT ALSO INHABITANTS OF TIRFEYNE WHO ARE VISITING EARTH: FAIRIES, GENIES, LEPRECHAUNS, PIXIES, GREMLINS, TROLLS, GNOMES, ET CETERA. THE ONLY THING NEEDED TO FIND AN INDIVIDUAL IN A SCOPE IS TO KNOW THAT INDIVIDUAL'S NAME. THERE IS BUT ONE BLIND SPOT IN THE SCOPES: THEY CANNOT PENETRATE EARTH'S SURFACE TO SEE UNDERGROUND.

Orville Gold, genie historian of Feyland

Tired and reeling, I felt burdened with both the weight of the indigo bottle and the weight of Laz's words.

What *was* this extra magic, this Feynere power? Why had no one else ever mentioned it? Not even Meteor had come across it in his studies; if he had, wouldn't he have suspected something when I told him how my magic behaved?

I would rather have heard it from Meteor.

How could I be a Feynere? It seemed dangerous. When I'd turned the cloak into aevum derk, I had drained myself of almost a million radia without knowing it. Was there any way to control it? Maybe I should have asked Laz that question. No. If I had, he would have sensed my weakness. How I wished he didn't know so much about me. Remembering his sneer, I was tempted to steal his cap and cast a forgetting spell on him. But if I did that, wouldn't I be as bad as Lily Morganite? Let him go his troggy way, and I would go mine.

Carrying the indigo bottle was like travelling with the end of the world hanging around my neck. I had to get rid of it. I didn't dare keep it in my home any longer. The rooms apart from the hearth room might still be safe, but what if Lily found a way to widen the opening in my protections?

I had made the right decision, refusing to give her the aevum derk. She must never, never get hold of it! Now, where could I hide the indigo bottle so no one – *no one* could take it?

Of course, I thought of Earth.

Yes, Earth, that place of gentle breezes and lovely trees, that fascinating land of humans – Earth could hide the aevum derk. I could bury it there. Not even fey scopes could find anything in the human world once it was underground. And though I would normally need to be invisible to escape the view of the scopes myself, last week I had created a spell to ensure that no magical means could find me, no matter where I happened to be.

I loved Earth. Loved it with an unreasoning and helpless affection that drew me when it shouldn't. Yes, I, Zaria, was Earth-struck. I didn't know why, I only knew that I loved the human world from the moment I first beheld it through the visor of a fey scope. That day, I had crossed through a portal for the first time, risking painful penalties and worse. And after that first visit, nothing could persuade me to stay away.

I suspected my mother felt the same. She had never spoken of it, of course, but she didn't have to. The painting in her room told me. I had even tried to write to her about it, in the letter I never finished.

Though it's unlawful for a fairy of fourteen, I've been to Earth more than once. I would hesitate to confess it, but I believe you will understand. The painting in your room shows a forest on Earth.

You love the human world as I do, don't you?

Have you ever been friends with a human, Mother? Ever watched a human in secret, longing to know more about him? I have. Not as a godmother-in-training might do; something else entirely.

That was as close as I had come to telling anyone about Sam Seabolt, a human boy not much older than me. We'd met only a short while ago, but it seemed that I'd known him much longer than a few weeks. None of my fey friends knew what he meant to me, though Meteor might have guessed. Even Sam himself didn't know – not after I put him under a forgetting spell. If he ever saw me again, he wouldn't know me. But though I had made sure he would remember nothing of me, I could never forget *him*.

My friends wouldn't understand. They would blame me for being drawn to a human at all, for seeking his friendship, and for wishing he could remember me now. I didn't want to be condemned. Not by them. And even more important, I didn't want there to be any possible chance for Lily Morganite to learn that a human was important to me. Not that my friends would tell her voluntarily, but Lily's magic had a long reach.

I had hidden my visits to Sam as best I could, and I didn't think she'd ever seen us together. If she had, she wouldn't hesitate to hurt him.

And now I was going back to Earth, but I wouldn't allow

myself to seek out Sam Seabolt again. No, I had spied on him for the last time. I would go straight to a grove of trees on a ridge above a field of wild grass. I'd been there before. There, at the base of a tall blue spruce, I had buried my mother's spellbook to keep it from Lily Morganite. Most important, I had cast a long-lasting spell: no one but me could disturb the ground there. Ever. I could bury the indigo bottle in that same spot. It would be safe, and I wouldn't have to spend more radia on another enchantment.

Now that I had a plan, I felt slightly less dazed and terrified and tired. All I needed was to cross over to Earth. I should have snooped around Laz's café looking for a portal. Everyone knew that smugglers had portals; Laz probably had one leading straight out of a room in the back of the Ugly Mug. How else could he run all those Earth goods? He was too stingy to pay someone else to smuggle for him.

Then again, if Laz had a favourite portal to Earth, it probably led somewhere I didn't want to go. Maybe into a sweetshop or a place that stored coffee beans, somewhere across the world from the grove with the enchanted ground.

Yes, I'd be better off travelling through a portal I'd used before. So, I transported to the Golden Station, the great hub from which most fey travellers made their journeys to and from Earth.

* ★ *

It was the middle of the night; I'd never been to the Golden Station so late. As a fourteen-year-old fairy, it was against the law for me to be there, no matter what the time of day, so I tried not to attract attention.

Symbols etched the walls, part of the durable spells holding open the portals to Earth. Hundreds of fairies and genies were flying in dozens of directions inside the vast marble room. Hallways branched off it, and each hallway held dozens of portal doors. Judging by the noise, the portals were getting lots of use, clicking open and slamming shut every two seconds. They showed no signs of failing as the Gateway of Galena had failed.

The fey folk were all talking so loud I couldn't tell what anyone was saying. Besides, I was focused on the hordes of gnomes marching up and down and watching everyone. There seemed to be far more of them than usual, and I feared that some of them could be Lily's minions. Were they simply keeping order, or were they looking for me?

Laz had said my disguise was terrible, but I hoped it would be enough to fool the gnomes. Head down, my newly dark hair hiding most of my face, I flew to a familiar door in one of the smaller hallways. I had found this portal by chance on my first journey to Earth. It got very little use by other fey folk, so I thought of it as mine. And I had given it a silly name: the Cornfield Portal, because it led to a cornfield on the other side.

Now, rising eagerness flooded across my wings as I opened the door. No one seemed to notice as I stepped through to Earth.

Spikes of rain pelted me, so thick and fast I could hardly breathe. In moments I was soaked and shivering. And the field on Earth had changed. The corn was cut, leaving only a stubble of dead stalks. Miserably, I hovered, longing for somewhere safe and friendly, somewhere dry and warm.

I thought of Sam Seabolt's quiet street, of his wooden house painted green with a white trim. How thankful I was that I'd never told anyone where he lived. No one knew, not even Leona. And at this hour, Sam and his family would be asleep. I could get out of the rain and wait for the storm to pass. They'd never know I was there.

It was too much to resist; all my resolutions about keeping away from Sam dissolved. I hurried to transport away from the rumbling thunder, the wild lightning and rain, and instantly found myself in Sam's room.

The first thing I did was to take off the bag holding the heavy bottle and set it on the floor. Then I looked at the human boy. A streetlamp outside shone over his red-gold hair, so colourful it could have belonged to a genie. He slept soundly, though his window was open a little. Wind blew in, riffling pages of a book that lay on the floor.

Water ran from my hair, my wings, my gown. It dripped more with every shiver of my wings. Quickly I infused to

Level 7. 'Dry me,' I whispered. It would be more magic lost, but worth it.

The water evaporated. Very quietly, I slid the window closed and looked around. Shelves lined one of the walls, holding books and narrow boxes and shiny statues. Clothes lay on the floor; a shirt was flung over the back of a chair.

I floated towards Sam and hovered lightly, listening to his breathing, wondering what it would be like to live in a world where technology took the place of magic. Suppose I had been born a human girl? I loved to visit Earth, but would I want to live here? Could I accept being unable to fly or use a wand?

Sam had basic magic. If you didn't count flying, he had more than Andalonus; he had enough to go through a portal. I had seen him do it. When it happened, I didn't feel surprised. After all, everyone knew that the occasional human had Level 5 magic.

'Do you have above Level Five?' I whispered. Humans weren't given crystal watches, so there was no way to know the answer.

The rain was softening. I could hear it running down the window, a steady slide of water, gentle as a lullaby. How tired I was. If I went to sleep now, maybe I could step into Sam's human dreams, and tell him all that had happened since we last saw each other.

No, I must not sleep. If I did, I wouldn't wake until morning and lose my chance to bury the indigo bottle during the night. It wasn't wise of me to come here. Seeing Sam – even asleep – only awakened my wish to befriend him again.

No one must know of my visit, least of all Sam himself.

Chapter Fifteen

Feyland is ruled by King Oberon and Queen Velleron (sometimes called Mab), However, they do not enjoy managing the day-to-day governance of their kingdom, and so they turn it over to the High Council of Feyland. There are twelve councillors: six fairies and six genies, all of whom begin their service with radia reserves of green or above. The leader of the Council is called either Magistria or Magister, depending upon whether that leader is a fairy or a genie.

The royal rulers live in the sapphire stronghold on Anshield Island. By means of passwords that open the gate, all councillors have access to the stronghold. If ever Feyland is in distress, the councillors inform the king and queen, who come forth and do their utmost to aid their subjects.

Orville Gold, genie historian of Feyland

Reluctantly I glided away from Sam's bedside, and as I did I caught a glimpse of myself in a small mirror on the wall.

I didn't like looking at my disguise, not at all. I wasn't sure why, because Sam was asleep, so there was no one here to see it but me.

I just wanted to look like myself.

I waved my wand. 'Take off my disguise.' Immediately the streetlamp showed my wings purple again, and my hair its normal shade of lavender.

Drifting closer to the shelves along the wall, I examined them. A small bottle lay on its side. Picking it up, I let the light from the streetlamp play over it. It was made of plain amber glass covered with a fine layer of dust. When I unscrewed the cap, the bottle was empty. Perfect for my purpose, something the boy had obviously forgotten. It would never be missed, and I wanted a memento of Sam. More importantly, I needed it for another reason.

This was a safe place, quiet and still. Here, I could transfer a little aevum derk from the large bottle to the small one. Leona and Laz had convinced me that the powder was a mighty weapon. After burying most of it, I would keep just a small bit on hand in case of dire need.

I rubbed the little bottle on my gown to dust it before setting it on the windowsill. The cap was made of plastic, which would never do for aevum derk – thanks to Laz, I knew that now.

Lily had created a glass lid for her cup, but I would be more clever. It would take less magic to transform something than to make something from nothing. Infusing my wand, I touched the plastic cap. 'Change into glass.'

I brought out the indigo bottle and set it carefully on the sill. How heavy it was, its dark shine more terrifying than ever. The powder it held could kill off the magic in an entire region of Feyland. What if I spilled it? If one small grain touched my skin, what would happen to me?

I had to stop thinking about what could go wrong. Otherwise, I might as well live out my days in a hideaway, doing nothing, seeing no one.

I glanced at the bed, where Sam remained lost in sleep. Lucky for him, he had no idea who was in his room or what I'd brought with me.

For a second, I thought of Laz, but only because I happened to know that he had somehow been selected to be Sam Seabolt's genie godfather. Not that he took his post seriously in the least. I had even heard Laz scoff at the idea that humans needed fey folk for anything, especially to help them grow up. But just then I wondered if Laz had ever checked in when Sam was a baby or a young boy.

I wasn't about to ask him.

'Unseal,' I said, tapping the indigo bottle with my wand.

With the greatest care, I poured aevum derk from one bottle to the other. My wings fluttered as I hurried to seal both of them with my strongest magic. 'No one but me can open or break these bottles, for ever and always.'

Tucking them into my bag, I slung it around my neck and took a last look at Sam. 'Goodbye,' I whispered.

Of course I wanted to stay with him. But instead I transported to the grove.

The only sound came from dripping trees, the night so dark I could see only black outlines of the grove. Kneeling on the soggy ground next to the blue spruce, I felt large drops spattering me. I was cold again, and damp. And so tired.

I dug with my hands, which were soon coated with mud and crumbling pine needles. After a while, I lifted out my mother's spellbook and used the sleeve of my gown to wipe some of the mud away.

Unlike the aevum derk, Cinna Tourmaline's spellbook felt light, almost weightless. Holding it again, I breathed easier.

Now that I knew I could use common words for spells, I wouldn't need to memorize those my mother had recorded. A normal fairy would study every spell until she knew them all by heart, but I wasn't a normal fairy. Still, the words on the pages were precious to me, because my mother had written them. I hugged the book, and while I did, she didn't seem so far away. I could actually imagine finishing the letter I'd been writing her.

'I'll write it all down,' I whispered. 'And I will find you and free you.'

Wrapping the spellbook in scarves, I stowed it in my bag. Then I dug deeper, and brought up something else I had buried: a human weapon, a laser gun – the very same gun that had injured Leona. I was tempted to take it too because I had seen its deadly red beam. Such a weapon could keep me safe from Lily's followers. Even a crowd of gnomes carrying iron bats would not be able to hurt me if I raised this human gun against them.

But I left it under the tree with the indigo bottle. I couldn't bear to be the first one to bring a gun into Feyland. Bad enough that I had created aevum derk, a dreadful weapon of magic.

I had done what I could now. The aevum derk was hidden beneath the blue spruce. Hidden well, and even if someone happened to learn where it was, no one could remove it but me. My long-lasting spell would make sure of that.

I placed the little bottle of aevum derk deep in a pocket of my gown. Yes, I would carry it with me, although I knew just how dangerous it was. I had kept it from Leona, afraid she'd get hurt or cause disaster. Shouldn't I keep it from myself too?

Maybe so. But somehow risking a friend seemed much worse than risking myself. Besides, I was more careful than Leona. Not by much, some would argue – but I would never blow up a human's house and turn him into a toad as she had done, no matter how much he offended or hurt me.

By now, I was shivering and faint. The thought of returning through the gnomes in the Golden Station was daunting. If I didn't get some sleep, I could easily make a mistake.

I decided to sleep there in the grove. Crawling under the prickly spruce branches, I called on my magic again to make a trench that held warmth, and pillowed my head on the lumpy bag holding my mother's spellbook.

Chapter Sixteen

No trees grow upon the world of Tirfeyne. There are many tall bushes, and a great variety of flowers, most of which can also be found on Earth. Our homes are built of stone and precious metals, not wood. Paper comes from the pounded stems of reeds – unless, of course, it is smuggled here from Earth.

Our world is rich in minerals and gemstones. Tirfeyne also holds a great variety of insect life and birds. However, there are no beasts – unless gremlins or trolls were to be counted as beasts.

Orville Gold, genie historian of Feyland

'We'll find it here.' The voice cut through my sleep like a claw raking my ear. A sweet voice, but sharp and hard. *Lily Morganite.*

My eyes flew open. Daylight filtered through the blue-green needles of the spruce branches around me. The thick branches dragged on the ground, but through them I could see dainty feet in jewelled slippers hovering just above the earth.

Instantly I whispered the spell of invisibility and then held still.

'How can you be sure?' Another voice spoke in tones too low to distinguish. A set of genie boots joined Lily's feet. I noticed that the boots were green and rather new.

'Zaria Tourmaline is predictable,' Lily answered. 'She seeks out the same places if she is fond of them.'

'But—'

'The powder will be here, Councillor. Here, where she believes it will be safe.'

Councillor! Which councillor? I strained to hear more. Please, please, I must not give myself away. And the bottle *was* safe. My spells were unbreakable. No one but me could disturb the ground here. Ever.

The genie tapped one ankle with his opposite foot. 'Those who are looking through the scopes did not report seeing her on Earth.' He was whispering now.

'She eludes the scopes by casting spells of invisibility.'

'Impressive.'

'Do not be impressed,' Lily told him. 'Be glad. Every time she casts invisibility, she is fifty radia poorer.'

A pause before he whispered, 'She could be watching us now?'

'No,' Lily said. 'Invisibility must be renewed every ten minutes. Even Zaria is not so reckless that she would squander three hundred radia an hour to stay in this world. Besides, her next move will be to learn what she can about the powder. Mark my words, she is back in Feyland searching for knowledge.'

The genie's feet almost touched the ground. 'Why haven't you been able to track her?'

Who was it? Who among the High Council of Feyland was working with Lily Morganite? If only he would speak up. I squinted hard, but the tree branches blocked my view of where he hovered, and I dared not move.

Silence for a moment. I could imagine Lily frowning. 'She must have found a spell to mask herself.' Her voice brightened: 'At her present rate, in a few months Zaria will have used up all her radia. She will be powerless.'

'Until then,' the councillor said, 'can you afford to gamble?'

'Watch me,' Lily answered.

She knelt beside the spot where I had buried my deadly treasures. Through a small gap in the spruce needles, I could see her as she reached into her gown for a cup I recognized – a cup of smoky glass covered with a lid.

I pressed both hands to my mouth as Lily snapped off the lid, upended the cup, and shook it over the ground. She smiled. 'There is just enough powder to destroy the magic protecting this spot.'

I should have done something. I should have leaped up and used all the rest of my radia. Anything to stop her. But I was frozen, truly frozen with terror. I could not think; I could not move. I lay curled in the trench, my hands over my mouth.

She began digging with a shining silver trowel. Lily moved fast, ladling clumps of rotten needles and dirt. Reaching into the hole, she took out the indigo bottle. She cradled it as if it were a dear child, then stowed it in a pouch fastened to her gown.

She reached into the dirt again. As she brought out the laser gun, she gave a tinkling laugh. 'Oh, Zaria,' she said. 'You *can* surprise me.'

She put the gun into another pouch, then dug for a while before she grunted in disgust. 'She has taken the spellbook.'

Without warning, she waved her wand and spoke the transport spell. '*Transera nos.*' Then she disappeared along with the councillor before I could blink.

My wings were fluttering so hard, they rattled the spruce branches.

'She has it,' I sobbed. '*Lily Morganite* has the aevum derk.' How did she know about this spot? She must have spied on me even more than I had guessed! I hugged my mother's spellbook and cried, repeating over and over, 'She has it. She has the aevum derk.'

And what did *I* have? A few pinches, sealed in a small amber bottle.

At last I crawled out from under the blue spruce branches; I flew back and forth where the grove met the fields. The place was deserted, the grass lying flat and brown, trampled by last night's wind and rain.

And then I remembered. I had sealed the indigo bottle. Lily couldn't open it or break it.

Lily had said herself she had only enough powder to destroy the magic on my spot. Not even her gnomes would be able to break my spell. They had not been able to get past the magic I'd laid on my house.

'I will take back the bottle,' I said.

How?

Where would Lily hide the aevum derk, and what did she *want* with it? When she stole it, she meant to use it. For what? And how angry would she be when she couldn't open it?

Oh, how badly I wanted to see my friends. Taking the bottle from Lily seemed impossible, but maybe together we could come up with a way. The four of us working as one had overcome all twelve members of the High Council of Feyland, and Lily Morganite was only one fairy.

One fairy with swarms of followers. One fairy with billions of radia in her personal reserves. One fairy with a full bottle of aevum derk.

I couldn't get back to Feyland fast enough. My friends weren't planning to meet up again until evening, but I couldn't wait; I'd track them down using enchantments if that's what I had to do.

From the fields near the grove, I transported to the

Cornfield Portal. The sky glowed like azurite, as if it had never known a storm. But where my fey eyes should have shown me a doorway to my world, there was nothing. Nothing but shorn cornstalks collapsing into mud.

The portal was closed!

'She doesn't want me to pass this way again,' I whispered. 'Me, or anyone else.'

How did Lily know which way I'd come? And how was I going to get home?

I'd either have to search for a different portal or create a new one. Both would take more radia.

In a few months Zaria will have used up all her radia. She will be powerless. Again I was following Lily Morganite's plans for me, like it or not.

Chapter Seventeen

FEY MAGIC IS MUCH MISUNDERSTOOD BY HUMANS;
HUMANS SEEM TO BELIEVE THAT MAGIC CAN SOMEHOW
TURN ASIDE PHYSICAL FORCE. THIS IS UNTRUE. FEY FOLK
ARE JUST AS VULNERABLE TO PHYSICAL INJURIES AS HUMANS
ARE; MAGIC CANNOT SAVE US FROM BLADES, BULLETS OR
EXPLOSIONS. WE CAN USUALLY MOVE FAST ENOUGH TO
DODGE KNIVES OR ARROWS, BUT ONLY THE VERY SWIFTEST
AMONG US CAN AVOID A BULLET.

Orville Gold, genie historian of Feyland

I decided against looking for the nearest open portal. I
didn't know how much radia it would take to find it.
Besides, I couldn't know in advance where I would end up
once I stepped through an unknown portal. For all I knew,
Lily had used some of her vast stores of radia to create a
portal nearby. It could easily lead, not into Feyland, but to
some other region of Tirfeyne. My protections might be
powerful in Feyland, but I doubted they would help me if I
landed in Troll Country.

I'd need to create a portal of my own, from a place Lily
Morganite wouldn't suspect.

Again, I thought of Sam's house. Maybe it had a room that no one used, a room that would be a good place for a portal. It would be worth checking, at least.

I glanced at the sun. It was still early, but not so early that some humans wouldn't be awake. I mustn't be seen. Out of habit, I spoke the traditional spell of invisibility. '*Verita sil nos mertos elemen.*' Another fifty radia gone.

Invisible, I transported back to Sam's room.

The bed was empty. Silently I glided out through the door. I heard dishes clinking, and followed the sound down the hall. Sam and his little sister Jenna were sitting at a wooden table in a sunny room. They looked cosy there together, Jenna's long braids red–gold like Sam's curls.

Their mother poured brightly coloured juice into tall glasses. 'Drink up, you need to be out of the door in fifteen minutes,' she said.

'I don't get it,' Sam said. 'Why can't I just go with Dad and see the comet dust? It's not like it would hurt me to miss a day of school.'

The slender woman turned to the stove. 'University policy. No outsiders. You know that.'

'I'm not an outsider; I'm his son.' Sam slid a glass towards his sister.

'The security is massive,' his mother said. 'Why can't you just be proud that your father is one of the few people in the world who gets to touch that comet dust? And be happy he's well enough to work again.'

85

'I am,' Sam answered. 'That doesn't have anything to do with—'

'Drink your juice,' his mother interrupted.

'What would comet juice taste like?' Jenna giggled.

Sam's movements were quick and sure as he frowned at his mother, smiled at his sister, then drank from his glass. I wanted to hover there watching until they left, but it was also very painful to be spying on this human family. There were four of them, although the father wasn't in the room. Four – the number my family should have been. I'd been only a few years older than Jenna when I lost so much. And my brother Jett had been about the age that Sam was now.

I mustn't linger. Much as I'd have liked to stay, I had to get back to my friends in Feyland, had to find a spot for my portal.

On my right was a stairway leading down. It was too narrow to allow my wings to expand, so I braced myself with the banister and took the stairs awkwardly on foot, glad of the carpet covering them; it muffled the sounds of my steps. The air began to smell a little musty as I descended. At the bottom of the stairs was a plain door. I opened it, and found myself in a large room with a grey floor and walls. I recognized the texture of concrete.

There wasn't any furniture. Machines stood along one wall, but the opposite corner held nothing but shadows and cobwebs. A perfect spot for a portal. Untouched.

I floated straight to the wall and then stopped,

remembering. I had once *sealed* a portal, and it had taken a thousand radia. It had also called for an elixir of troll magic mixed with honey from Earth. What would it take to *create* a portal?

I set my tote on the dusty floor and took out my mother's spellbook. The advanced spells would be towards the end. I turned the pages till I found the one I sought.

CREATING PORTALS TO EARTH

Requires Level 75 magic and 1000 radia. Durable spell, needs to be refreshed every two hundred years.

Select a deserted location or construct a barrier on the portal (see Barrier Spell). Any solid substance can be used for a portal, including stones, walls, or the ground itself.

Spit upon the portal spot. Touch it with the tip of your wand. Infuse the wand to Level 75. Speak: 'Chantmentum upana portalis nos Erthe.'

I almost laughed with joy. No troll elixir. No honey. Only spit from a Level 75 fairy or genie. I was a Level 100 fairy, so I could achieve 75 without effort. The thousand radia would be a lot to lose, but I had expected no less.

I read the spell over again. 'Creating portals to Earth,' I said. 'Creating portals *to* Earth.'

To wasn't the same as *from*. Could I open a portal to Feyland from the Earth side? And if I could, where should it lead? Although I would like to connect Sam's house to my own home in Feyland, I could still hear Lily's voice: *She seeks out the same places if she is fond of them.*

Not this time. This time I would go against what I wanted to do. It would be much safer for Sam's family, anyway, to open a portal to a remote part of Feyland where fey folk were unlikely to blunder into it – and where Lily would have no reason to look. However, I had no personal knowledge of most of Feyland, especially the remote places. Only a few weeks ago, I had made my first trip to Oberon City. Before that, I'd lived my life inside Galena, sheltered land of children and parents. Sighing, I realized I'd have to make up a spell that opened a portal to an unknown place. What if it wasn't possible to create a portal from Earth, a world whose inhabitants had so little magic?

Sighing more deeply, I accepted that I might waste a thousand radia on a spell that didn't work.

Chapter Eighteen

PIXIES ARE AN ODD RACE. THEY HAVE THEIR OWN LANDS, AND EVEN THE TROLLS RARELY ENCROACH ON THEIR TERRITORY, FOR IT IS KNOWN THAT PIXIES HAVE A SPECIAL SORT OF MAGIC THAT CAN LURE OTHERS AWAY FROM THEIR DUTIES.

PIXIES ARE FOND OF MUSIC AND DANCING; IT IS ALL THAT THEY LIVE FOR. THEIR BONES ARE LIGHT AND WELL SUITED TO THE MANY HOURS THEY SPEND GYRATING. THEIR THROATS ARE LONG, WHICH ALLOWS THEM TO WARBLE ALL DAY. THEY DO NOT EVEN SPEAK UNLESS IT IS WITH SONG.

Orville Gold, genie historian of Feyland

I listened for a full minute to be sure no one else was nearby. Then I spat on the wall in the corner of Sam's dusty basement. I infused my wand to Level 75 and set the tourmaline tip against the concrete wall. 'Open a portal from here to a remote part of Feyland.'

Magic moved through my wand. When I put my hand against the wall, I felt no resistance. I had done it!

'Give this portal a barrier so no human may find it.' I had to do that spell. Had to. Sam had enough magic to pass through a portal. He must not slip into Feyland again.

'Goodbye, Sam,' I whispered to the wall. And stepped through it.

My new portal led to a hilly place where the grass grew as high as my waist. A breeze carried scents I hadn't smelled before, delicious scents that reminded me of sage plants and rosemary flowers.

I crested a hill and searched the horizon, but saw no buildings, only more hills covered with long grass. Drifting along, I felt like a plumed seed, with no idea where I was.

I turned to go back. I should have marked the portal. Why hadn't I? Now the waving grass all ran together. I hovered, twisting my dirt-streaked skirts in frustration. There was nothing to tell me which hill I had seen first among all those around me.

'Alloo?' called a piping voice.

I whirled round to see someone about my own height, gently swaying with the wind. Her arms were green like the grass surrounding her, and her hair was pink. She looked at me with eyes that shifted colour like water, mostly blue. Happy eyes.

'Lost, are you?' she sang. Her voice was as delicate and delightful as the scent wafting around her.

She fitted everything I'd heard about pixies, except her eyes and her voice. Beryl had told me pixies had eyes like smugglers, shifty and sharp – and voices that could flatten a troll.

'Lost, lost?' she sang again.

'Yes,' I answered, wondering why I didn't feel worse about it.

Smiling, she beckoned. 'Follow.'

She turned and weaved through the grass. For no good reason, I did as she asked and followed her. Although she didn't fly, she was very fast; I had to pump my wings to keep up as she led across more hills. Every so often she would wave to me, pointing ahead. Somehow, all that seemed to matter was keeping her in sight.

I began to hear music. Flutes, lyres and drums, and also many voices singing. How joyful they sounded, and free of care. Hearing them, I wished for nothing more than to keep listening.

Flying past yet another hill, I saw a wide meadow below. All across it figures swayed, bending and turning. Their colourful heads looked like dancing flowers. Music poured from dozens of instruments, mingling with the voices.

My guide had brought me deep into Pixandelle.

Every young fairy and genie is told to stay out of Pixandelle. Beryl had warned me over and over about what lay in store if I ever let myself be tricked by pixie wiles. She said pixies led travellers astray whenever they could.

I must have stepped out of the portal on the very borders of Pixandelle and Feyland. But there had been no sign of it being a border zone. Had another durable spell failed? Weren't the borders supposed to be infused with magic?

And yet, I had never been alerted that I was leaving Feyland. Why hadn't I considered all this sooner?

The drums of the pixies pounded my ears with pleasant rhythms while their misty fragrance made my head spin. I wished the music would stop for a moment, just long enough to let me get my bearings.

It didn't. It got louder, gathering me in. It seemed to form into a sparkling shield around me, protecting me from all my sorrows, easing my troubles. I heard words in the melody now:

'*Dance for ever, for ever dance . . .*'

I floated to the ground, and the pink-haired pixie ran to my side.

'Dance, dear fairy, dance upon the air,' she sang, her voice blending with the music swirling around us, her smile warm.

She wanted only what was best for me.

What if there was nothing wrong with being here? What could it hurt to take a few minutes to dance one song? I smiled back at the pixie, who urged me closer to the drummers. My arms moved in a flowing motion; my feet twirled, and my wings caught the currents of the breeze. I felt light and free, happier than I had been since . . .

For ever.

Chapter Nineteen

PIXIES DO NOT NEED TO CAST SPELLS, FOR THEIR MAGIC IS IN MUSIC AND DANCING. THEY CAN MAKE EVEN THE MOST STRONG-MINDED FEY FOLK FORGET THEIR DUTIES, FORGET THEIR FAMILIES, FORGET THEMSELVES.

Orville Gold, genie historian of Feyland

Something was tapping my forehead. 'Wake up, Zaria,' said a harsh whisper. 'Wake up.'

'Mmph,' I mumbled.

'Wake *up*.'

Opening my eyes, I saw a face close to mine. Silvery eyes, dark hair, worried frown. Leona. Just behind her hovered Meteor and Andalonus. All three wore ugly necklaces that looked like they'd been strung with gravel. Dull leaden pendants hung on their chests.

Leona poked me again with the tip of her wand. I brushed it aside and tried to snuggle down farther into the soft grass. My head was resting on my tote bag, and I was comfortable.

Leona slipped a necklace over my head; it was just like the one she wore. Instantly I felt sad and afraid and unbearably tired. I wanted to take off the necklace, but when

I tried, Meteor pried my fingers off the strand. Not gently.

I couldn't do much more than lift my head. 'What are you doing here?' My voice rasped as if I'd been screaming for hours.

They didn't answer.

A group of pixies was surrounding us, singing and swaying. They didn't seem kind any more, didn't seem wonderful. I wanted them to go away, but they were moving closer.

Meteor picked me up off the turf. My body ached everywhere; my wings were limp.

Leona touched us. '*Transera nos.*'

I was in the nest in my mother's room, squished against Meteor, with Leona and Andalonus across from me. Meteor got out of the nest, and helped me prop myself up with pillows. My joints seemed filled with grit, and so did my eyes.

'Pixandelle?' Leona said.

I groaned.

'I'll get you some water and sonnia.' Leona flew out of the room.

'Why?' Meteor asked. 'Why *there*?'

I stared at him, remembering. The portal. The aevum derk. Lily Morganite.

Leona returned with water. I gulped it. She handed me a bowl of dried sonnia flowers. They tasted so good!

'How did you find me?' I asked.

'When you weren't here for our meeting,' Meteor began, 'we decided something must have happened to you.'

I frowned. 'We're supposed to meet this evening.'

A pause while they shook their heads.

'You danced longer than you planned,' Andalonus said. He looked frightened, as if he thought a band of pixies might break through the walls and carry me off.

'We were supposed to meet the day before yesterday,' Meteor explained.

I tried to remember. I had begun dancing . . . It had been morning. I'd felt so blissful. Were there times when the day had darkened?

'Two days and nights with the pixies?' I croaked.

'We looked everywhere for you,' Meteor went on. 'Couldn't find a trace.'

'We were afraid Lily had snared you somehow,' Leona said.

Snared. It was too close to the truth. How was I going to tell them she had the aevum derk?

'Leona had the idea to track down Laz,' Andalonus said. 'He's the one who told us a young fairy with violet wings had been seen among the pixies.'

My eyes snapped to Andalonus's face. '*Laz* told you where to find me?' I struggled to sit up. 'How much did it cost you?'

'A thousand radia,' Meteor answered. 'Leona paid him.'

'I'm so sorry.'

'He also warned us that if we went into Pixandelle without sorren charms, we would fall to the pixie magic ourselves.' Leona lifted the ugly necklace over her head and held it at arm's length. 'Meteor bought one for each of us.'

I didn't want to ask how much Laz had charged for the charms. Poor Meteor! It would be bad enough to hand over radia to anyone, but to Laz, whom he despised?

'And he told us we'd better race as if trolls were after us to get you out,' Andalonus continued, 'because any fairy who spends more than a few days with the pixies isn't able to leave them.'

I pulled the charm from my neck and examined it. The pendant was shaped like the heel of a foot, and the beads were only lumps of clay. I set it on the pillow next to me, hoping that taking it off would make me feel better.

It didn't.

'Thank you for coming after me,' I said. 'I'm so sorry . . .' How long had they been awake looking for me?

'Zaria,' Meteor said slowly, 'what happened? How did you end up in Pixandelle?'

Sighing, I tried to focus, my mind in freefall. I pushed myself up higher in the nest so I could unfurl my wings. 'I flew off course.'

'Obviously,' Leona said. 'Tell us, Zaree.'

'You might not stay my friends when you hear what I've done.'

But I told them, starting with my visit to Laz.

'*Laz?*' Meteor interrupted, his hair actually bristling. 'You told that smuggling trog about the powder? You asked *him* what it was?'

'Why shouldn't I ask him for what he knew? He's the one who put the cloak on me,' I said.

Leona shook her head at Meteor. 'Let her talk.'

So I did. About the aevum derk. And about being a Feynere. They listened, fascinated. Meteor asked the most questions about the aevum derk. And the instant I said the word 'Feynere' he drummed his head with his hands.

'Of course, of course!' he exclaimed. 'A Feynere. That's what you are. It explains everything: spells out of common words, magic rising up, the power of your enchantments . . . everything.'

I thought of what Laz had said: that he expected a Feynere to look grand and powerful. *Not a smallish fairy with rather plain colouring*. It bothered me that Meteor might have felt the same way, but I didn't want to bring it up.

He was frowning now. 'Lazuli knows about you being a Feynere?'

I nodded. 'He knows.' My wings drooped. 'I wish he didn't, but he does. I swore him to secrecy – it was the best I could do.'

Andalonus put a comforting hand on my shoulder and then tilted his head at Meteor. 'I'm curious, O sage one: if the Feynere have such unsurpassed powers, why is Zaria's level lower than Leona's? Why does Leona's watch register a level higher than anyone else's in Feyland?'

Leona smiled at that. 'Yes, Meteor. Why?'

None of us had ever seen Leona use her full power, though I suspected she had poured it into a futile spell to try to heal her mother. The human laser gun had burned her mother too, but of course all Leona's magic had not been able to help. And since then she had shown no desire to tap Level 200.

Most of the time, I forgot what a powerful fairy Leona was. But her level was twice that of any on record for living fey folk, equal to the strongest fairies and genies who had ever lived.

'Yes, Meteor,' I echoed. 'Why?'

Meteor sighed. 'Feynere magic isn't measured in levels. Leona, when we first talked about Zaria's spells, you said she must have something else, and you were right. Feynere magic goes beyond levels. It's different.'

'So I'm still the highest level?' Leona asked, grinning at me.

Meteor nodded, and I grinned back at Leona.

'If it's so different, why does Feynere magic use up radia?' I asked, a bit peevishly.

'Because it's still magic,' Meteor answered. 'And it's still fey.'

Chapter Twenty

In Feyland, the understanding of time itself is part of our heritage as fairies and genies. Long ago, when we travelled freely between our world of Tirfeyne and the human world of Earth, we taught humans to make timepieces and to follow the hours. Not that they remember this, or give us the honour we are due. Nor do they recall that it was fey folk who first showed humans how to construct snug homes as well as grand architecture. For millennia, we have helped them in a hundred thousand ways that now go unrecognized. Their historians have forgotten. This is due in part to the Edict of the Unseen. According to the terms of that edict, fairies and genies allow only the youngest humans to see us. If sighted by a full-grown human, we must cast a forgetting spell at once. And wise fey folk that we are, a thousand years before the Edict was enacted, we became cautious about being seen. (I do not count leprechauns among the wise.)

Orville Gold, genie historian of Feyland

It took a while to tell my friends the rest of my news. At first, they were too shocked to take it in. But finally they understood: Lily Morganite had the aevum derk. She couldn't open it. I'd kept a small amount in reserve. And I'd created a portal that happened to lead to the edge of Pixandelle.

Leona seized on how I'd kept some of the powder. 'You should use the last of it on Lily! Right away, as soon as we can find her.'

When I argued that Feyland needed Lily's billions in stolen radia, Leona scoffed.

'She won't use it to benefit Feyland!' she yelled. 'What if she uses it to open the bottle of aevum derk?'

My heart ached along with my head. 'But kill her?' I whispered. With Lily dead, how would I ever find my family?

'She'd happily kill *you*,' Leona answered. 'Why spare her after everything she's done!'

'No, Zaria's right,' Meteor told Leona in his calmest voice. 'If Feyland loses all the radia Lily controls, we would be weakened for ever.'

'We're *already* weakened,' Leona fumed. 'Tell her, Meteor.'

'I looked at Meteor. 'Tell me what?'

'Things are bad,' he said. 'More of the durable spells have begun to fail.'

'I know,' I replied. 'At the border of Pixandelle and Feyland, there weren't any alarms, nothing to warn me.'

He nodded glumly. 'When we were looking for you, we went to the Golden Station and found pandemonium. The portals have closed.'

'What? All of them?'

'We didn't check every single one,' Leona snapped. 'But it looked that way, yes.'

'What about all the fairies and genies who were on Earth?' I cried. 'How will they get home?'

Meteor shook his head, striped hair falling into his eyes.

Trapped on Earth with no way back! Even an Earth-struck fairy or genie would be desperate to get home. Those who could create a portal were few and far between. Level 75 was rare among fey folk, and so was a thousand radia.

I had thought Lily guessed which portal I used, and closed it to spite me. But if every portal in the station had failed, maybe Lily hadn't closed the Cornfield Portal after all; maybe the durable spell keeping that portal open had simply failed along with all the others. But why would she let the portals fail? Did Lily hate Earth just as Beryl had hated it? Did Lily despise humans as Beryl had done?

'And as if that's not enough, many of the viewing stations are having trouble with their scopes,' Leona added.

I sat with my wings huddled around my shoulders. What

was happening to my beloved Feyland? And what would become of the connections between human and fey, so long cherished, and now at risk?

The pause was long and awkward, broken by Andalonus. 'I have news too,' he said. 'I found Lily.'

I stared at the blue-haired genie.

'You know her hiding place?' Leona leaned towards him.

'She isn't hiding,' Andalonus said. 'She's flaunting herself as an outcast, giving speeches to anyone who will listen.'

'You went *after* her?' I asked. 'But she knows you're friends with me and Leona. What if she had gnomes on the lookout for you?'

'I had a disguise.' Andalonus mussed his frizzy hair, looking proud.

'Did Leona enchant you?' Meteor asked.

'You don't have to use magic to be in disguise.' Andalonus pulled on his ears. 'I covered my hair with a cap, smeared my face with dirt, and kept in the background so no one would notice me.'

'You ingenious genie,' Leona said. 'Do you know where she's staying?'

'In some old falling-down tower on the edge of Oberon City,' Andalonus answered. 'She's got gnomes repairing it fit for royalty. And she makes speeches from the balcony.' He waggled his eyebrows. 'She goes on and on about how the king and queen aren't fit to rule, and the councillors are even more bumbling and selfish than the king and queen.'

Bumbling and selfish. It felt odd to be in agreement with Lily. My friends and I didn't have a good opinion of the High Council of Feyland. As far as we were concerned, they were a bunch of rotten trogs.

I wondered if King Oberon and Queen Velleron, safe on their Island of Anshield, had heard the news of the failing durable spells and the chaos in their kingdom. Surely they would soon leave the sapphire stronghold and help us?

'Lily's like a queen to her followers,' Andalonus was saying. 'And she's promising to give them radia too. She says they'll each get a thousand more.'

'But Lily doesn't give away magic!' I cried.

'She's lying, of course,' Leona said impatiently.

'She talked about something called *aevia ray*,' Andalonus said.

'What's aevia ray?' I asked.

'It's a fabled powder,' Meteor answered. Obviously he knew something the rest of us didn't. As usual. 'It's supposed to generate new magic. But it's impossible to make.'

'It can't be impossible,' Leona argued, 'or you wouldn't be able to study it.'

'The main ingredient is dust from a comet's tail,' Meteor said. 'And since history began, anyone who's set out to ride a comet has never come back.'

I tried to get up, but flopped back on the pillows.

Andalonus turned to me. 'Zaria? What's wrong?'

'Lily might be able to get comet dust,' I said faintly.

Meteor snorted. 'Even if she had ten trillion radia, she still wouldn't have the power to ride a comet.'

'What if she could get the dust on Earth?'

'What?' Meteor asked softly.

'Humans,' I said. 'I think the humans have some comet dust.'

Chapter Twenty-one

THE HUMAN LIFESPAN IS QUITE SHORT COMPARED TO THAT OF FAIRIES AND GENIES, WHO USUALLY LIVE TWO HUNDRED YEARS OR LONGER. SOMETIMES, LONG-LIVED FEY WILL ATTAIN TWO HUNDRED AND FIFTY YEARS. HOWEVER, FAIRIES AND GENIES REACH PHYSICAL MATURITY AT A RATE SIMILAR TO HUMANS, ALLOWING US MANY MORE DECADES TO ATTAIN WISDOM.

THE NORMAL FEY LIFESPAN DOES NOT PERTAIN TO KING OBERON OR QUEEN VELLERON, WHO LIVE ON THE ISLAND OF ANSHIELD, WHERE TIME TAKES NO TOLL UPON THE LIVING. FEY RULERS WOULD BE IMMORTAL EXCEPT THAT THEY SOMETIMES LEAVE THEIR STRONGHOLD.

Orville Gold, genie historian of Feyland

I was so exhausted, I poked my forehead with the tip of my wand to wake up. 'Meteor,' I said, 'tell us everything you know about this aevia ray.'

'Zaria,' he said, '*why* do you think humans have comet—'

'I can't tell you,' I interrupted sharply.

'Why not?' he asked.

'I overheard something while I was on Earth. It doesn't matter where I heard it, does it? All that matters is that Lily might be able to get hold of it.'

Leona was giving me a questioning look, while Andalonus bobbed beside her.

'Please, Meteor. Tell us what you know?' I was desperate for him to stop asking questions; I didn't want to explain about Sam.

Meteor sighed. 'I already have.'

I leaned forward. 'Then you've got to find out more. Please, Meteor. If Lily wants it, we have to learn about it.'

'All right,' he said quietly. 'I'll research it.' He drew his wand. 'Will you be here when I come back?' He wasn't looking at Leona and Andalonus; he was looking at me.

'Where else would I be?' It wasn't exactly a lie. I did plan to be there – if I could do what I needed to do in time.

'*Transera nos.*' Meteor disappeared.

Too tired to think, I closed my eyes, only for a minute.

When I jerked awake, Leona and Andalonus were on my mother's window seat, murmuring to each other.

Dragging myself out of the nest, I expanded my wings. 'How long have I been asleep?' I demanded crossly.

Andalonus gestured at the window. The light outside told me it was well into afternoon.

'Blasted pixies, curse them all,' I said. 'Where's Meteor?'

'Still gone,' Leona answered. 'And now that you're up, you'd better change your gown, Zaree. That one you're wearing is even more hideous than those sorren charms we got from Laz.'

I looked down at my skirts, which were hardly better than rags and smeared with dirt. Leona was right. Hurrying to my own room, I found a gown that wasn't quite as wrinkled and was much cleaner.

Back in my mother's room, I picked up the pixie charm and dropped it over my head. Among the pillows where I'd slept, I found the tote bag holding my mother's spellbook. I crammed the book into a cupboard. 'Cinna Tourmaline's spellbook cannot be stolen,' I said, dousing the cupboard with magic.

'What are you planning, Zaree?' asked Leona.

Sometimes I wished she didn't know me so well. I didn't like cutting her off; it wasn't something I'd normally do. But I didn't want to get into an argument with Leona Bloodstone about going to Earth.

So I transported away without answering her.

Laz spotted me the moment I crossed the threshold of the Ugly Mug. For once, he wasn't involved in a game. I watched in irritation as he glided across the room towards me.

'This way,' he said when he reached my side.

I followed him past a nearby curtain into a dim hallway

and through a creaky door. The room we entered was small and crammed with crates. Goods from Earth, no doubt. Being with Laz in an enclosed room was enough to bring on some very bad memories.

He was wearing his leprechaun cap, so there was little I could do to him, but I drew my wand anyway.

'Returned from the pixies, I see,' he said. Then his face turned serious. 'Dangerous for you to be here, Zaria. For you, and for me.'

'Why?'

He shook his grey-blue head. 'You may be a Feynere, but nothing can save you from carelessness.'

'I'm not careless!'

'Oh?' His gravelly voice had risen a notch. 'You're here without even attempting a disguise.' He tapped his temple. 'Acting foolish.'

'I'm here because I need to use your portal to Earth. Where is it?'

A flash of surprise crossed his face and then he pulled a dull expression. 'Portal?' As if he didn't know what I meant.

'Just tell me.' I gripped my wand tighter. 'I have to get to Earth. Now!'

'Why not take the portal that brought you so close to Pixandelle?' He stared pointedly at the charm around my neck.

My portal! Did Laz know *everything* that happened in Feyland?

'I wouldn't be able to find it,' I snapped. 'It's not marked.' *From the Feyland side.*

'Sorry. Unlike you, I know where *my* portal is,' he said. 'But no one else does. And that's how it's going to stay.'

I shook my wand. '*Your* future depends on my getting through safely.'

Laz clicked his tongue. 'You don't say.'

Raising my wand high, I infused it and pointed at a tall stack of crates. 'I hear coffee smells gruesome when it gets over-roasted.'

'So it does, so it does.' The genie put up a hand. 'No need for a display, Zaria.' He stood, his calculating eyes on my wand.

'And I will *not* pay you a toll,' I said, wand still poised. I was quite willing to blow up not only all the coffee barrels in this room, but everything else the smuggler might hold dear.

He must have sensed my mood, because he stopped resisting. 'Follow me.'

Chapter Twenty-two

SONNIA IS THE ONLY FOOD THAT FEY FOLK REQUIRE FOR HEALTH AND STRENGTH. IT IS OFTEN PICKED FRESH, BUT IT MAY ALSO BE DRIED AND STEEPED AS A TEA. HOT TEA, WELL BREWED, IS A PLEASURE ENJOYED NOT ONLY BY FEY FOLK, BUT ALSO BY THE MORE INTELLIGENT SPECIMENS OF THE HUMAN RACE. AND THOUGH MAGIC HAS NO WORTH WHEN IT COMES TO HELPING A HEART THROWN INTO DESPAIR, A STOUT POT OF TEA MAY BE BENEFICIAL AT SUCH TIMES.

Orville Gold, genie historian of Feyland

Laz took me into another small room. We squeezed past several barrels to wedge ourselves into the only open corner. He gestured at the wall.

'Where does it lead?' I asked.

'Storage space. In a basement,' he answered.

'Does it have a barrier against humans?'

'Nothing but the best.'

I mumbled my thanks and then stepped through the portal into a large room with cement walls. Stray cobwebs hung from solid wooden beams in the ceiling, but the rest of the place was clean, and well lit with electric lights. The air smelled like Laz's café: warm, rich and heady. *Coffee*. Of course.

Bags and barrels lined an aisle wide enough for my wings to fan out comfortably. Sucking in a large breath, I waved my wand. 'Take away my wings till I ask for them again.'

The change was sudden, and I stumbled sideways, steadying myself against a big barrel. I could hear footsteps from above, small thuds coming and going on the floor over my head. But the basement room was empty of people.

I infused my wand again. 'Make my skin a human colour and dress me in human clothes.' I wanted to pass for human, and my lavender skin and fairy gown would get in the way. After all, human beings didn't have the variety of skin colour that fairies and genies did. Also, the human girls I had seen did not wear soft gowns that flowed around their ankles.

My magic delivered faded blue trousers, a soft black shirt and grey jacket, and bouncy shoes with laces. Looking at my hands, I saw that my skin colour had changed to one of the standard human shades – like the cocoa Laz had served to Meechem. I tucked the sorren necklace inside my shirt. No human would find it appealing.

Smiling a little, I slid my wand into an inside pocket of the jacket, and practised walking up and down. Without my wings for balance, I shuffled awkwardly and had to clutch at coffee barrels, but after a while I got all the way down one of the aisles without holding on.

I turned down a different aisle. The barrels in this one had been opened; lids were fitted loosely over the tops. I lifted one of the lids and saw a scoop among the shiny beans. Curious, I dipped my hands in the barrel. The aroma of coffee grew stronger.

A nearby door banged open, and a tall man hurried through it. His dark skin reminded me of Meteor's, but he didn't have striped hair or green eyes; his hair was short and black, his eyes deep brown.

When he saw me, he gasped. 'What the——? What do you think you're doing?'

I pulled my hands out of the barrel and stood unsteadily.

'A little young to be stealing, aren't you?' he asked.

'I'm not stealing!'

The man advanced on me. 'Oh? Then what're you doing down here, punk?'

I spread my hands to show him they were empty. 'Nothing.'

'Nothing? You expect me to believe that?' He whipped out a small black device and tapped it with a finger.

'It's true!' I cried.

The man held the device to his ear. 'Yeah, Jim, call the police. There's a kid down in the storage room . . . Yup . . . *Girl* . . . Yup.' He slipped the thing into a pocket and took a step closer, peering into my eyes. 'You high?'

'High?' I asked. *No. My wings are gone, and I'm standing on the floor.*

'Purple contacts, eh? Who you workin' for, kid?' He shook his finger in my face, his voice loud. 'All this time, merchandise disappearing and we have no clue who's taking it. Looks like we'll find out now. And if you tell me how you've been knocking out my cameras, I might go easy on you.'

I backed away from him.

'Hey,' the man asked. 'You hurt?'

'No.'

'Why're you limping?'

'I'm not.' I took another step backwards and staggered into a shelf. A big barrel tipped towards the floor; I barely had time to get out of the way before it fell. The lid popped off. Coffee beans streamed out, jumping across the floor as if alive.

'You *are* high.' The man reached for me. I tried to slither away but my feet slid on the spilled beans.

'Stop right there, young lady!'

What else could I do? I pulled out my wand. '*Transera nos*,' I said, and visualized the porch outside Sam's house.

Standing by Sam's front window, I peered inside. No movement. I thought by this time in the afternoon some of the humans would be home, but I was wrong.

The leaves of the tree in the front yard were turning red

and orange; a few had fallen to the ground. Stepping off the porch to pick up one of the leaves, I admired its pattern and the yellow veins running through it. I brought it to my nose and sniffed the delicious spiciness of Earth.

Warm thrills travelled over me at the thought of seeing Sam Seabolt in daylight. Not only would I see him, but if everything turned out as I hoped, I'd get the chance to talk with him for a while in my human disguise.

When we'd met before, he couldn't feel natural around me; he was too nervous about talking with a fairy. First, he thought it meant he was losing his mind and 'seeing things'. And when he began to believe in me, I couldn't stay visible for long because I knew Lily Morganite might be looking for me in the fey scopes. All our conversations had been short and fraught with danger. But today, it would be different. Today, maybe I could get to know him the way a human friend would do.

I mustn't wait for him on his front porch, that much I knew. After all, I would appear to be a stranger, and human strangers didn't make a habit of waiting for each other like that. I would go out to the street, and then when he came home I would walk towards him.

Starting down the walkway, I fumbled a little for balance. I stood on the pavement near his house, my eyes roaming over the human neighbourhood. I barely had time to admire the tree across the street with its brilliant yellow leaves before I saw Sam walking towards me. Forgetting to pay attention to my feet, I fell. If I hadn't been wearing a jacket, I would have torn my skin.

'Are you OK?' He bent and offered me a hand.

I took it, and instantly felt pleasant heat run down my arm. 'Thank you,' I gasped as he pulled me up.

He blinked. 'Do I know you?' He seemed to be looking at the top of my head more than at my face, but I was looking at all the beautiful colours in his eyes: the amber, the hazel, and the brown lit with gold.

'I'm Zaria,' I answered.

His eyes met mine, and he said, 'Whoa. Are those purple contacts?'

'Uh,' I answered.

'Zaria. I'm Sam. Do you live around here?'

'Yes,' I lied.

'Just move in?'

'Yes.'

He smiled in a welcoming way. 'You going to Coyote High?'

I nodded hesitantly. Was I giving the right answers? The word 'high' seemed to be a favourite with humans, and yet they were unable to fly without the help of machines.

Sam smiled more warmly. 'Sophomore?'

With no idea what he meant I nodded again, suddenly wishing Laz were standing invisibly at my shoulder so he could guide me through these strange human customs. With all his journeys to Earth, he would surely understand.

'That must be where I've seen you,' Sam said. 'But you're not in any of my classes, are you?'

I shook my head. 'I'm interested in comets,' I said, hoping I wasn't breaking social rules.

He lifted one eyebrow. 'You like comets?'

'Yes.'

Sam gave a short laugh. 'You don't look like an astronomy geek.'

Astronomy geek?

'That's OK,' he told me, smiling. 'I'm a geek too. And my dad's one of the best exobiologists in the world.' He sounded proud.

Exobiologist. This was a human word I didn't know. 'I heard about him,' I said, trying to cover my ignorance.

'Yeah?' He squinted at me suspiciously. 'You know my last name?'

'Seabolt.'

He gave me a considering look but seemed a little pleased too. 'Did you read about my dad online?'

If I'd had my wings, they would have fluttered. *I overheard you when I was invisible.* I looked at him, unable to think of an answer. I didn't even quite understand the question, and I was seized with fresh anger that fey children didn't learn about modern humans. Many of our teachers hadn't even been to Earth in fifty years!

But Sam overlooked my lack of reply. 'My dad's so lucky – he gets to see the comet dust up close. Did you hear about how they brought some here for his team to analyse?'

I nodded, but felt alarmed. 'They didn't bring *all* of it?'

'Nah, they had to share it around.' He shifted his feet but his eyes never left my face.

Would Lily Morganite know about this? 'Where else did they take it?'

'I think some of it's at a lab in New York. A few other places.'

'What other places?' My voice was beginning to squeak.

Sam shrugged. 'Have you Googled it?' Another human word I didn't know. 'I could help you with a search, but I'm starving.' I was sorry to hear he was so hungry. He looked a little thin, but nothing unhealthy. 'My house is right there.' He pointed, and seemed to be waiting for me to say something.

I spoke softly. 'Are you asking me to visit?'

Sam tilted his head. 'Are you from a foreign country?'

'Yes,' I said. 'I'm from a different land.'

'Which one?'

I was feeling so confused, I told him the name of my world. 'Tirfeyne.'

'Hmmmm. Never heard of it.' He didn't wait for me to answer. 'So d'you want to come over? We could get some food and do a search.'

Search? His house?

I nodded. Maybe once we were inside, he could tell me how to find the dust.

'Don't you have to call your mum?' Sam asked.

I shook my head, hoping my face wouldn't show my sadness.

'Wow,' he said, 'she doesn't make you check in, and lets you dye your hair that colour? Awesome!'

I picked up a lock of my hair and held it in front of my eyes. Same lavender sheen as ever, dull by fairy standards, but I suddenly remembered humans didn't grow hair 'that colour'. Theirs could be only four shades: black, brown, yellow, and the occasional red – unless they used dyes.

Sam watched me. 'What's wrong? Don't you like your hair? My sister would kill for hair like that.'

'She would?' I gasped. From what I'd seen of Jenna, she was a good-tempered child. I didn't think she'd want to kill anyone for anything, let alone hair. Was Leona right about humans? Did all of them – even the children – have a tendency to violence?

Sam chuckled. 'Nice acting! Are you into theatre?'

'Uh . . .' I began to understand he wasn't serious about his sister. But why would he joke about killing?

He started up the steps to his porch, moving fast. Attempting to keep up with him, I stumbled again. I recovered but felt like a fool.

'Did you hurt yourself when you fell?' he asked, putting his hand on my arm.

'Nothing terrible.' Carefully I set my foot on the steps and hoped he would keep touching me.

'You look like you're limping.'

'I can't walk very fast yet.'

His eyebrow lifted again, and he kept his hand on my arm.

Chapter Twenty-three

TEACHERS OF FEY CHILDREN ARE OFTEN IGNORANT OF CHANGES ON EARTH. REGULAR VISITS TO EARTH ARE NOT REQUIRED, AND ASIDE FROM A BASIC HUMAN CULTURE CLASS, CHILDREN ARE NOT TAUGHT ABOUT HUMANS AND THEIR CUSTOMS.

THEREFORE IT IS NOT UNCOMMON FOR ADVANCES MADE BY HUMANS TO REMAIN UNKNOWN TO LARGE PORTIONS OF THE FEY POPULATION. MANY FAIRIES AND GENIES ARE UNAWARE OF THE EXTENT TO WHICH HUMAN TECHNOLOGY HAS BEGUN TO RIVAL OR EVEN TO EXCEED FEY MAGIC. FOR INSTANCE, HUMANS CAN NOW COMMUNICATE WITH EACH OTHER INSTANTLY, REGARD-LESS OF HOW FAR APART THEY MAY BE, AN ACHIEVEMENT SURPASSING FEY ABILITIES. AND THEY HAVE CREATED MANY FANCIFUL TOYS FOR THEIR CHILDREN.

Orville Gold, genie historian of Feyland

Sam's hearth room had two beige couches and a big chair so puffy it could have been a nest. Little tables stood on the ends of the couches and on either side of the chair.

Reaching into his pocket, Sam pulled out a red object that I'd seen him use on my very first visit to Earth. He tossed it to me. As I caught it, he asked, 'Do you want to use my phone to search while I get us food?'

I had no idea what to do. We had studied telephones in Human Culture class, but if this was a phone, my teachers had been behind the times about what they told us. As usual. And this 'phone' made me nervous. It had caused me no end of trouble the last time I'd seen it.

I held it out to Sam. 'Would *you* search?' I asked.

'Sure, if you want.' He took back the phone then touched the front, making a small screen light up. 'Comet dust,' he muttered, and pressed some keys under the screen, which flashed. Letters began to appear. To me, it looked like magic.

'Got it!' He stood next to me, holding the phone so I could see words roll up the screen as he talked. 'Besides New York and CU, some of it went to Harvard. Stanford. Some to the University of Chicago. They loaned a little to Munich. Oh, and Oxford.'

I tried mightily to remember my Earth studies, but I didn't know those places. 'Do you have something I can write on?'

'I could just send you the links. What's your number?'

Links? 'I'd rather write it down.' I hoped I didn't sound as bewildered as I felt.

'OK.' He handed me his phone and walked into the next

room. Returning with a pad of paper, he gave it to me along with a pen. At least these things were familiar to me. My mother's writing desk held a small stash of paper. And as for human-made pens, although they were banned in Feyland, everyone knew they were much easier to use than quills.

'I'm gonna get a snack,' Sam said. 'Want anything?'

'No, thank you.'

When he left the room I studied the little screen. It was like looking at a page in a small book, except the letters were lit up. The words 'comet dust NASA Exlander' repeated several times. I didn't know how to make the words move as Sam had done. When I tried pressing buttons, all the letters vanished.

I could hear Sam opening cupboards and handling dishes. It wouldn't take him long to come back. Drawing my wand, I pointed it at the phone. 'Show me the locations of the comet dust.'

The screen flashed, and the list of names and locations came back. Stowing my wand, I began writing. I enjoyed the steady, even flow of ink from the pen.

I was taking down the address of the last place on the list when Sam came in carrying a plate piled with food. 'You sure you don't want anything?' he asked.

I shook my head, and Sam dropped onto the couch beside the table. He patted the seat next to him. 'Sit.'

Clumsily, I did. It felt good to be with him in his human

home, behaving like a human girl. I offered him his phone. Setting it on the table, he smiled then took a big bite of food.

I ripped the piece of paper from the pad. 'Thank you.' I folded it, wishing I could stay all afternoon.

'Anytime.'

'It didn't say how much total dust there is.' I tried to watch him without staring.

'I don't know the exact number of grams or anything,' he said, 'but it's, y'know, about as much as the tip of your thumb. That's what my dad said, anyway.'

That's all? 'Do they keep it guarded?'

'Oh yeah, tons of security. The scientists have to sign for it and pass a clearance – all that stuff.'

Pass a clearance? I felt muddled. On Tirfeyne, valuable items would be locked in iron and watched by gnomes. Or placed with the king and queen inside the sapphire stronghold on the Island of Anshield. 'Oh,' I said.

'Yeah, the rocket they sent into the comet cost about a zillion dollars, so they're really careful with it, y'know.'

Of course. Humans had used their technology to fly into a comet and bring some of its dust back to Earth. I didn't doubt they were careful.

Sam looked wistful. 'It'd be awesome to get that close to something that's flown all over the solar system. Wish I could. But they won't let me near it, even though I'm Dr Seabolt's son.'

'I'm sorry,' I said. I'd like to grant his wish. All I'd need to do was visit Sam once I had stolen some of the comet dust. But how would I explain what I'd done? He would know me for a thief — a thief who would steal from his father.

I should go.

I had what I needed now. Much as I longed to stay beside Sam, time was passing. I had to get to the comet dust ahead of Lily Morganite. And if I didn't go now, it would only become more difficult to leave, because every minute I spent with Sam he seemed more fascinating. I wasn't sure why. It was like being enchanted.

I stood up carefully so I wouldn't fall over. 'Thank you for helping me.'

'Going already?' He stood too, and I could hear his breath, a little quicker and louder than it had been a few seconds before.

I wished I could explain that I was trying to stay ahead of an evil fairy. 'I'm late.' I stuffed the list of locations into a pocket in my Earth trousers.

'Too bad.' Sam picked up his phone. 'Can I snap a pic? For my sister.'

I put both my hands up, furiously shaking my head no.

'Camera shy?' He sounded surprised.

'Yes,' I said firmly.

He put the phone down. 'It's fun talking to a girl about

comets,' he said, and his face turned a little red. 'Especially a girl with purple eyes.'

I smiled. 'It's fun talking to a boy with eyes full of amber light.' I wanted to touch his cheek and I didn't stop myself. The minute I reached out, he did too and put his hand over mine. I could feel the pulse in his palm against my skin, and I wanted to kiss him, though I knew such a thing was absolutely forbidden.

Pulling back, I turned for the door.

'Do you want me to walk you home?' Sam asked. 'Where's your house?'

'Not far.' *Depending on which portal you use.* 'But don't come with me.' It would be very awkward trying to keep up with my lies.

Looking over my shoulder, I saw disappointment in his face. 'OK, well, see you around,' he said.

I opened the door. 'Goodbye,' I said, longing to stay.

Chapter Twenty-four

THE TRANSPORT SPELL IS ONE OF THE GREAT ACHIEVE-
MENTS OF FEY MAGIC. THIS SPELL CAN MOVE EITHER AN
OBJECT OR A PERSONAGE ANY DISTANCE INSTANTLY. THREE
THINGS ARE REQUIRED FOR A SUCCESSFUL TRANSPORT.
ONE, THE DESTINATION MUST BE CLEARLY HELD IN MIND.
TWO, THE ONE CASTING THE TRANSPORT SPELL MUST KNOW
EXACTLY WHERE HE OR SHE IS. THREE, THE TRANSPORT
CANNOT CROSS WORLDS.

A TRANSPORT SPELL USES LEVEL 8 MAGIC. THE
AMOUNT OF RADIA NEEDED DEPENDS UPON THE VOLUME OF
THE OBJECT OR PERSONAGE BEING TRANSPORTED. THE
WORDS OF THE SPELL ARE '*TRANSERA NOS.*'

Orville Gold, genie historian of Feyland

In case Sam was watching, I walked down the pavement
from his house and around the corner, feeling terribly
clumsy. My breathing was so rapid it was as if I had been
flying fast for miles and miles, and I could still feel Sam's
hand over mine. Waves of warmth poured down to my toes,
warmth that turned to shivers of regret. What had I done?

I had used the one human I cared for most; used him to

tell me what I needed to know so I could steal from his father and his world.

But I didn't want to use him. No, not at all. I wanted to be his friend.

More than his friend.

I stopped under a cluster of aspen trees growing near the pavement. Their leaves dangled like thousands of slim pendants; I would have liked to fly into the branches and rest there for a while.

If only I could leave the dust alone. If it hadn't been for Lily Morganite, I could. Why did she have to seize every single thing in her path that might make her stronger? Wasn't she strong enough already?

Since meeting Lily, I had turned into a thief and a liar. I had become someone who sought out troggy smugglers and took advantage of innocent humans. What would become of me as I continued to fight her?

Maybe I should stop.

But if she got control of even more radia than she already had, there was no telling what she'd do with it. I had to keep the comet dust away from her.

Ducking behind the aspens, I restored my fairy form and repeated the spell for invisibility. Then I took out the piece of paper with the list of locations. Did Lily know where the dust had been taken? If so, she might already be raiding these places one by one.

If she could find them.

I could gather the comet dust by transporting to each place on the list. But a transport spell would not work unless the destination could be held clearly in mind. And of course, I had never been to any of the places where the comet dust was being kept.

Would my Feynere powers allow me to transport to the address of a place I'd never seen? And suppose I *could* do it – what if Lily were looking for the same spot? At a hundred years old, she must have taken many journeys to Earth, maybe even more journeys than Laz. She would know how to find what she was after.

What if I ran into her?

I studied the first address on my list: the University of Colorado.

If I cast a Feynere spell and it didn't take me where I wanted to go, would it take me somewhere else? For all I knew, it would flatten me into the piece of paper I held. I'd be locked away like those who had been stuffed into the genie bottles of old, unable to leave unless a human with minimal magic found me somehow and triggered the spell to release me.

'Hush,' I told myself, and infused my wand to the transport level. 'Take me to the comet dust at the University of Colorado.'

Immediately I was standing in a clean room. The lighting was strangely harsh: bright, yet cold. White countertops had been scrubbed so many times they looked worn and faded.

Greenish walls held framed documents, and a sharp, rather unpleasant scent I could not identify hung in the air.

Two people were in the room with me.

I recognized Sam's father immediately. Tall, with fiery red hair that clung to the back of his neck. The last time I had seen him was through a fey scope looking out from my world. He had been in a hospital bed recovering from a broken arm, a blow to the head, and a mysterious case of amnesia. He might well have died if I hadn't helped him recover his memory.

Yes, my fondness for Sam had led me to break another law of the fey. It's not as if I didn't pay attention to all that Beryl had taught me. I knew it was forbidden to take any magical action on behalf of a full-grown human. I knew that we fairies and genies were allowed to cast spells *only* for the benefit of our own godchildren until they turned sixteen. It wasn't Beryl's fault that I broke the laws she taught me; not her fault I went to Earth the first chance I found, long before my godmother training could begin.

When Sam asked me for help finding his father, how could I say no? I, who knew what it meant to lose a father, to live without him, to wonder what had become of him!

I still didn't know how or why Michael Seabolt had been hurt, but I suspected mischievous fey folk had been involved. It seemed likely, because my spell had reversed his memory loss. If the amnesia had come from a physical injury, I could not have done anything about it.

And I didn't regret helping the man who stood in front of me now. His arm was still in a cast, and his head was neatly bandaged, but he seemed well otherwise. And he looked up as if he sensed my presence.

A wingspan away, a black-haired young man sat clicking keys in front of a screen like the one on Sam's phone, only bigger. He was typing. I knew about typing, though of course we fairies and genies didn't use machines to write.

The young man took his hands off the keys. 'Doctor Seabolt? What's up? You hear something?'

'Thought I did, yeah.' Michael tilted his head. There were sounds all through the room: a soft buzzing and whirring from the lights and the machines – and also my breathing.

I held my breath. Sam's father looked around for a moment, his hazel eyes sharper and harder than his son's. He shook his head. 'It's nothing. I'm just spooked. They tout the security on this stuff, but it's not all that great, if you ask me.'

He gestured at a vial next to his elbow. I stared at it. Inside was something resembling grains of sand.

The comet dust.

'Yeah, kind of weak.' The young man stretched his arms. 'Well, time to call it a day.' He typed a few more letters and then the screen in front of him went dark.

I exhaled as slowly and quietly as I could. Sam's father was carefully shrugging his shoulders out of a white coat, which he tossed in a bin.

I wanted to take the vial right then while no one was looking. But what if these men were blamed for the loss? It would be bad enough for them to find it missing the next day. So I waited while Michael placed the comet dust in a metal box with stout clasps. The young man watched, his brown eyes alert. He glanced at the clock on the wall before making notes on a piece of paper attached to a board.

Together, they unlocked a metal cupboard that had the sheen of steel. It took two keys, one from each of them. They shut the box in the cupboard and locked it again. Then they scribbled on the paper.

The young man smiled. 'We're out of here.'

Sam's father flicked a switch. The harsh lights went out, leaving only a dim bluish glow from a row of smaller lights on the wall.

The door clicked behind the two men.

I waited only a few seconds before going to the cupboard they'd locked. When I touched it, I flinched in pain. Steel was made partly of iron. Feynere or not, the iron hurt me. Somehow, the humans had chosen a container that would keep out fairies and genies. Others might be able to endure the pain of touching it, but no other member of the fey could break steel. I could. In a fit of anger, I had once turned a band of iron to dust.

Lily might be able to charm or deceive a human into opening the comet dust with keys. Or she might hover invisibly until they took it from its box. But her magic would be useless against the locks I faced.

I flicked the locks with the tip of my wand. 'Open,' I said.

The cupboard door swung outward.

I touched the box inside too, and repeated the magic. The clasps fell away.

Lifting the vial from its resting place, I examined it. Though small, it would be big enough to hold all the comet dust from the other locations too – unless Sam was wrong about how much total dust the humans had collected. Each place I went, I could transfer the dust into this one vial.

I hated stealing something so precious from the human world – something many humans had worked hard to gather. It didn't seem right. And when Sam heard the dust had been taken, would he think of me? I thought of his trusting eyes and open smile, and sighed.

Opening the vial, I sniffed the contents. The dust smelled unlike anything I'd ever come across – on my world or here on Earth. Smelling it made me feel both light and dark. The light rippled, roared and rushed; the darkness sifted, swirled, expanded.

And I had a sudden thought: *What if I used this dust to make some aevia ray myself?*

I gave a hop of excitement, and my wings unfurled. With a bottle of aevia ray, I wouldn't fear a fight with Lily Morganite. Her stolen stores of radia wouldn't make her

132

untouchable. If we had aevia ray, my friends and I could replenish the radia that had gone missing from Feyland. The durable spells could be restored. We could shower gifts on humans: delightful gifts such as musical and artistic talent, inventiveness . . .

Best of all, if my family had drained their stores of magic by fighting glacier spells, I could give them back their lost radia. I could even give them extra.

When I found them.

I stowed the vial in my jacket, then blasted the cupboard in which it had been stored until there was nothing left of it but curling bits of melted metal. It was my parting gift to Michael Seabolt. No human would be able to account for what had happened; Sam's father would not be blamed for such a thing.

Bursting with the need for action, I studied the paper in my hand. Infusing my wand, I touched the next address on the list.

'Take me to the comet dust at the University of Chicago.'

After Chicago, I went to New York University and then to the Harvard campus, picking up comet dust. At each location, I transferred the amount I found into the vial I had taken from Michael Seabolt.

Next, I headed to Oxford and Munich. In both those places I set off alarms, pulsing red lights and screeching sirens. The storage cupboards there were more elaborate too, though no match for my magic. I arrived after people had left things locked up for the night. By the time anyone rushed in to investigate, I was gone. My last collection point was Stanford University. It was earlier there, so I had to wait for the humans to leave. But once they did, I took their comet dust.

It cost me hundreds of radia to complete all the transports and stay invisible, but I did what I had set out to do. I had the comet dust, combined into one small vial, now nearly full. I had it all.

I checked the sorren charm around my neck before taking the Pixie Portal through Sam's basement back to Tirfeyne. The minute I came through the portal, I marked it in my mind so I could find it again, taking careful bearings. I didn't want to use up more Feynere magic locating it in the future.

This time, the rolling hills covered with grass and the scent wafting on the breeze did not overwhelm my senses. Far from it. If anything, I felt repelled. I was in no mood to spend two days and nights frolicking with a band of pixies.

I caught movement at the top of the hill. The pixie sentry, no doubt. Hastily I transported to my mother's room.

Chapter Twenty-five

PORTALS TO EARTH SHOULD NEVER BE CREATED LIGHTLY. A DOORWAY BETWEEN WORLDS IS NO TRIVIAL MATTER, AND TOO MANY OF THE FEY ARE WILLING TO FLOUT THE LAWS OF THE LAND TO BECOME SMUGGLERS. TO THOSE LAW-BREAKERS, A SECRET PORTAL IS WORTH MANY THOUSANDS OF RADIA, AND THEY WILL GUARD ITS LOCATION WITH STEADFAST PURPOSE.

Orville Gold, genie historian of Feyland

My friends were waiting, but they didn't exactly give me a delighted welcome. Andalonus was the only one to return my grin. Leona was apparently still miffed at how I'd transported away without giving her a chance to join me; she wasn't truly scowling, but then Leona Bloodstone didn't have to scowl to make her anger known. Her eyes had a slaty glint, a sure sign she was trying to control her temper. And though Meteor's face lit up for a half an instant when he first saw me arrive, he immediately frowned.

'You said you would be here,' he grumbled.

I spoke in a rush. 'I'm sorry, but I didn't want to waste

time. Listen to this – I have it! The humans really *did* collect comet dust. They used their technology and—'

'*You have comet dust?*' Meteor interrupted.

'Yes!' I brought out the vial and waved it. 'Every speck they had on Earth.'

Leona dropped her grudge immediately. 'Zaree, you're a wonder!'

'How did you find it?' Andalonus asked.

It wasn't easy to tell them how I'd gathered the dust without mentioning Sam, but that's what I did. I had to dodge two dozen pointed questions from Leona, but the genies didn't pry. Meteor seemed to understand I had secrets to keep. Maybe he also guessed the nature of those secrets, but if so, he said nothing. Andalonus just listened.

When I got to the point in the story where I thought of making aevia ray myself, both Leona and Andalonus got so excited at the thought of defeating Lily Morganite and restoring Feyland, they started zooming around the room yelling with glee.

But then Leona stopped in mid flight and turned to Meteor. 'There must be more to aevia ray than comet dust, and we don't know the other ingredients,' she lamented.

Meteor's emerald eyes looked newly polished as he smiled at her. 'Yes, we do.'

I leaped at him, and he scooped me into his arms. It was our turn to fly through the room together. We spun joyfully, and for a moment I might have been taking my first dance with the pixies, I felt so light and carefree.

Then Andalonus bounced in front of us. 'So tell us, O master know-it-all,' he said to Meteor. 'Are the rest of the ingredients for aevia ray as easy to get as comet dust?'

'Ha,' I said as Meteor and I floated to the floor and let go of each other.

'Oh yes, so easy,' Meteor answered. 'For one, aevia ray requires troll magic.'

I cringed.

'Not to mention the cooperation of gremlins and pixies,' Meteor continued. He flipped a scroll out of his robe. 'Here's the list.'

I took it and sat between Andalonus and Leona to read Meteor's neat script.

Aevia Ray
1. *Comet dust (cosmos)*
2. *Nectara elixir (trolls)*
3. *Gift of a biscuit (gremlins)*
4. *Song (pixies)*
5. *Something cherished (leprechauns)*

'Trolls, gremlins, pixies and leprechauns?' Andalonus snickered. 'Are you sure you're not missing anyone?'

I felt queasy. 'Nectara elixir? What's that?'

'It's something closely guarded even among the trolls

themselves,' Meteor explained. 'Something they reserve for their royals. They never let anyone else near it.'

Andalonus grinned. 'Yes, they do. If it's guarded, they allow *guards* near it.'

Meteor snorted.

Andalonus levitated. 'And what about the "gift of a biscuit"?'

'That one item on the list took me hours to decipher,' Meteor said. 'It didn't say biscuit – it said a lot of ancient gibberish about gremlin *treasure*. I had to look in eight different scrolls to be sure that this "treasure" was actually sweet flat cakes. Then I remembered it's well known gremlins like biscuits better than anything.'

Andalonus hooted. 'Not only a biscuit, but a gift!'

'Yes,' Meteor answered. 'A gremlin has to give us a biscuit. Voluntarily.' He looked so grave when he said 'biscuit' that I giggled, at which he frowned. 'Gremlins don't give up their biscuits, Zaria.'

'Well, the pixie song shouldn't be too hard to get,' Leona said. 'Pixies sing all the time, don't they?'

'But it's a special song,' Meteor said. 'They have to teach us, and then we have to sing it. I couldn't find the name of the song, so we'd have to get the pixies to give us the right one – if they remember it. This list goes back four thousand years.'

'Four thousand years?' I asked in dismay.

'Four thousand years,' Meteor repeated.

I glanced over the list again. 'Something cherished?'

'By leprechauns,' Meteor told me. 'And that's all I could find. No specifics.'

Andalonus put his feet on the ceiling and called to us upside down. 'I know what leprechauns cherish. Chocolate – and coffee too!'

Ignoring him, Meteor looked at me and Leona. 'Also, the spell for aevia ray takes Level One Hundred. And it uses five hundred thousand radia.'

'Oof!' said Andalonus. 'How much new radia does that create?'

Meteor smoothed the hair out of his eyes. 'It's said that even a few grains are equal to several million radia.'

I turned to Leona, who turned to me the same instant. We nodded to each other.

'It's a foolish quest,' she said, 'but if it means we can stomp out Lily Morganite, I'm ready.'

Andalonus dropped to the floor, thumping the spiral pattern of tiles. 'I can't add to your magic,' he said. 'But when it comes to foolish quests, I'm gifted.'

Chapter Twenty-six

GREMLINS HAVE AN INSATIABLE APPETITE FOR HUMAN-MADE BISCUITS, SO THEY ARE EASILY BRIBED BY GIFTS OF ASSORTED VARIETIES. IT IS FAR LESS TROUBLE TO ACQUIRE BISCUITS THAN TO LIVE NEAR GREMLINS, WHICH IS WHY THE HIGH COUNCIL HAS A TRADITION OF BRIBING GREMLINS TO STAY OUT OF FEYLAND.

GREMLINS DO NOT MAKE GOOD NEIGHBOURS. THEY DESPISE ALL FORMS OF PRODUCTIVE WORK. INDEED, THEIR DISGUST RUNS DEEP FOR ANY EXERTION THAT DOES NOT INVOLVE BREAKING THINGS. UNFORTUNATELY THEY HAVE AN INNATE UNDERSTANDING OF HOW PARTS FIT TOGETHER, MAKING THEM SKILFUL IN DESTRUCTION.

Orville Gold, genie historian of Feyland

Our mood switched from silly to sombre as we realized we were really going to seek out the ingredients for aevia ray.

'We should start with the pixie song,' Meteor said. 'Since we have sorren charms, we can get it without risking our lives.'

I disagreed. 'How will we get a pixie to teach us? We'd have to take off the charms to join the dance.'

Leona let her wings unfurl. 'You're not going, Zaree. You've already had two days with the pixies. I'll go.'

I looked at her injured wing. 'If you dance the way I did, you'll hurt your wing more.'

'I won't dance the way you did.'

Andalonus spoke up. 'I'll go with you, Leona.'

'I thought you were afraid of pixies,' she said.

'Not at all, not one teeny pitiful smidgen. Besides, I'm a great dancer.' Andalonus winked at Leona.

Meteor rubbed his jaw. 'It could work, but—'

'It *will* work.' Andalonus cut him off. 'It's a chance for me, the *un*gifted one, to help.'

'It's a wonderful plan.' Leona put her sorren charm around her neck.

'It is?' Andalonus floated just above the floor.

'Yes,' Leona answered firmly. 'Except that this necklace looks like a trog should be wearing it.' She asked to borrow one of my mother's scarves. Picking out a silvery one that set off her eyes, she put it around her neck to conceal the charm.

Then she waved a quick goodbye before transporting herself and Andalonus away.

When Meteor and I entered the Ugly Mug together, wax candles threw a dim, sultry glow, and the aromas of coffee and cocoa filled the air. A band of two leprechauns and three genies were beating drums of all shapes and sizes from big and booming to small and delicate. The rhythms tapped through my skin into my veins, mingling with the scents. Enchanting. I found myself wanting to order a large coffee, all for myself – and drink it. I *had* to stop coming here.

As usual, there was a wide mix of customers: fairies and genies, and renegade leprechauns who had escaped the Iron Lands. I noticed Meechem, the one who'd given up his magic cap, at a small table in the corner holding a steaming mug. Several more leprechauns were collecting empty cups and wiping down tables to pay off their bets after losing to Laz.

As Meteor took in the scene, he seemed unmoved by the delicious smells and pounding drums. He looked like he didn't trust his surroundings in the slightest.

Someone grabbed my elbow and swung me around. 'I told you not to come here in the open,' Laz hissed in my ear, and started pulling me towards a nearby hallway.

I didn't argue; after all, he was the one we'd come to see. I managed to seize Meteor's hand, and he came along with us.

Laz led us to the portal room, which was crammed with barrels of coffee beans. He touched a fey globe on the wall; it sputtered dully and then revived to cast a faint glow. Shutting the door, Laz perched on one of the barrels, wearing his leprechaun cap. It was the first time I'd seen him without a mug in his hand.

'What do you want this time, Zaria?' His murky eyes were half shut as usual.

'We have questions.' I perched awkwardly on another barrel.

Laz folded his bony arms. 'Well, I'm not one to turn down more radia,' he said. 'Same terms apply.'

Meteor floated up to sit on the tallest barrel. 'Terms?'

Laz gave a gravelly chuckle. 'Didn't tell your sweetheart, Zaria?'

'No, I didn't tell him . . . I mean, he isn't . . .' Keeping my eyes on Laz, I explained through gritted teeth: 'Meteor, this genie and I have an agreement: I get to ask him any question for fifty radia. *Anytime I want,*' I finished, glaring at Laz.

Laz nodded as if he had the upper hand. 'For one more day.'

'Fifty!' Meteor burst out.

I wouldn't look at him. 'So, *Mister* Lazuli,' I said. 'First question: How to bribe a gremlin?'

Laz's laugh turned into a cough. 'Biscuits. I'm surprised you don't know this already.'

'But suppose they already had biscuits. What would make them give them up?'

More sniggering. 'Nothing. Unless it was for a better biscuit.'

'What makes one biscuit better than another?' I asked.

Laz dragged his fingers through his stringy hair. 'If you wanted to bribe a gremlin, Zaria, and if you were a gambler – which, of course, you're not – I'd advise you to gamble on the chocolate chip flavour if you had only one choice. Though why you'd care one way or another is a puzzle.'

I hurried to ask my next question. 'What do leprechauns cherish?'

Laz leaned way back and peered at me with one eye closed. 'You've been here often enough to know the answer. They love things from Earth – especially coffee and sweets. Why?'

I exchanged glances with Meteor. '*I'm* asking the questions, Laz. So tell me, what's the best way past a troll guard?'

The genie threw back his head and treated us to a long, sneering guffaw. 'Troll guard. Good one.'

But when Meteor and I didn't laugh, Laz quit sneering. 'Wait,' he said. 'Getting past trolls? What do leprechauns cherish?' He muttered to himself – something about gremlin treasure – then pointed his wand at me. 'Aevia ray.'

Meteor froze. So did I. If we hadn't been so surprised, we might have been able to throw the smuggler off the scent, but neither of us could say a word.

'Aevia ray,' Laz hummed. 'I've been hearing it talked of lately; they say Lily Morganite is promising to hand it out like sonnia tea.' He clicked his tongue. 'But I know she doesn't have any. Yet.' His wand traced a circle in the air much too close to my face. 'You plan to beat her at her own game – don't you, Zaria Tourmaline?'

'Lower your wand.' I lifted my own.

'Of course.' He pocketed his wand and smiled a disturbingly wide smile. He leaped off his barrel and knelt on the dusty floor looking up at me. 'Allow me to offer you my services.'

'What services?'

'I'll throw in the questions I've already answered – for free.' He rose from the floor and floated up till we were eye to eye. 'You cunning little trickster. You stole the comet dust from the humans. Didn't you?'

I stared at him, too surprised to do anything but blink.

'We're leaving now.' Meteor's tone was full of disgust.

'So, you *did* steal the dust.' Laz flicked a lazy glance at Meteor and then focused on my face. 'When the Morganite looks for it and doesn't find it, believe me – you're going to need my help.'

Chapter Twenty-seven

EVERY HOUSEHOLD IN GALENA OWNS A FAMILY CLOCK, A
CHERISHED OBJECT THAT CHIMES THE HOURS WITH
CHEERFUL PRECISION. TO INSULT ANOTHER'S CLOCK IS
CONSIDERED AN UNFORGIVABLE RUDENESS.

Orville Gold, genie historian of Feyland

A coffee bean pinged against the floor, bounced twice, and came to a standstill.

Laz whipped out his wand. '*Revelum locat*,' he brayed.

Nothing stirred except my wings.

Laz began darting above the coffee barrels, jabbing at nothing. Meteor and I sat as still as we could, watching. Moving fast, Laz showed a very different side to the one I'd seen before. Gone were his normally slow, shuffling movements.

'Why did you perform a reveal spell?' Meteor asked.

'Thought we had a spy. Beans don't normally jump around by themselves.' Laz went to the door and examined the knob. He double-checked the lock, then squeezed into the far corner that held the portal to Earth. 'We should be going.'

'Going?' I squeaked.

'To Earth,' he said. 'To bribe gremlins you'll need biscuits, and I don't stock them here. No demand for them among fey folk.'

'But . . . couldn't a spy easily find you on Earth?' I asked.

'Scopes have failed,' he answered tersely. 'Didn't you know?'

'*All* of them?' Meteor asked.

'All. And even if that Morganite creature decides to repair one of them for her own purposes, she can't see past my cap.' He pointed to his head.

Meteor looked puzzled. I was surprised to hear Laz explain. 'My cap. Protects against magic. All magic, including the scopes. Or spells made by bad-tempered fairies – and genies.'

Meteor jumped from his barrel. 'Where did you—'

'Doesn't matter. What matters is *now*.' Laz glided closer to the corner.

'Uh,' I said. 'The last time—'

'Last time you botched everything. But I've messed up their cameras again. Nobody there this time of night anyway.' He gestured at the portal. 'I'll go first.'

He stepped through the wall.

'A portal? Here?' Meteor asked. 'A working portal, no less?'

'He *is* a smuggler.' I drifted towards the portal, but Meteor blocked me.

'What if he has Lily Morganite and a pack of armed gnomes on the other side of that wall?'

'He won't. He hates Lily.'

'Did that stop him before?'

'No. But then she double-crossed him.'

'And now he could double-cross you!'

I slid my hand into my pocket, checking the vial of comet dust and the little bottle of aevum derk. Both safe. 'Laz couldn't have known we were coming here tonight; we didn't know it ourselves till a minute before we arrived. Let's go. He's waiting!'

Meteor shook his head. 'I don't like it. How did he know about the ingredients for aevia ray? He doesn't look like any scholar.'

I eyed the portal. 'I told you, he knows things.'

'He could be working for Lily,' Meteor insisted. 'If we go through that portal after him, we should be invisible. Lily could repair a scope and use me as a way to track *you* on Earth, Zaria. And what if she's on the other side waiting for us?'

Andalonus might joke about danger, but Meteor wouldn't. What if he was right? It wasn't as if Laz could be trusted.

'Mind if I protect you with a spell?' I asked.

'Not at all.'

I waved my wand at Meteor. 'For the next month, you

cannot be found by any magical means, whether you're on Earth or on Tirfeyne.'

He bowed. 'Thank you.' His eyes moved to the portal. 'I'll go first,' he offered.

Chapter Twenty-eight

GNOMES ARE EXCELLENT WORKERS. THEY CLEAN, MAKE REPAIRS, SEW CLOTHING, DIG THE MINES, AND HELP TO KEEP ORDER. IN OTHER PARTS OF TIRFEYNE SUCH AS TROLL COUNTRY, GNOMES PERFORM OTHER JOBS – FOR EXAMPLE THEY MAY HELP HARVEST PUTCH, A SOMEWHAT SLIMY PLANT THAT FORMS THE MAINSTAY OF THE TROLL DIET. FOR THIS, THEY ARE PAID QUANTITIES OF FINELY GROUND GRANITE AND LIMESTONE.

Orville Gold, genie historian of Feyland

When we passed into the warehouse, no one greeted us with iron clubs. The place was dark and still, just as Laz had promised.

He guided us to a different building, an enormous structure filled with human wares but empty of humans. There, he pilfered three backpacks for us so we could carry biscuits more easily.

Next, we followed as he flew to a bakery, where the air was savoury and warm. Two walls of a large room were filled with shiny ovens stacked on top of each other. Along another wall stood big white tubs. And on the last wall, metal racks held dozens of biscuits. No humans were watching over them, though Laz assured us they'd return any minute.

'How many do we need?' Meteor asked.

'All of them,' Laz answered. 'The humans will blame each other and then bake more. So we'll take as many biscuits as we can carry.' He rubbed his chin. 'We want to beat the amount the Council gives the gremlins. Usually, the price for keeping them out of Feyland is two packets of stale biscuits a month – for a whole village.' He slapped a countertop. 'When we bring them *these* biscuits, we'll be instant legends.'

Meteor frowned. 'That won't make them *give* us a biscuit.'

'Yes, it will,' Laz answered. 'Good biscuits are to gremlins as gold is to humans. Humans seek favours by giving gold; why wouldn't gremlins give biscuits?'

Along with every other fairy, I had been taught that humans valued gold beyond anything, but I didn't believe it. In the time I'd spent on Earth, I hadn't seen any gold. I'd never even heard it mentioned.

'Let's get to it.' Laz hurried to scoop up biscuits and place them in paper bags we found stacked on a shelf. I helped him, quickly learning the different types. Ginger snaps were small and they stuck together, shortbreads were golden rectangles, snickerdoodles big and soft and fragrant, peanut butter very crumbly. As for the chocolate chip cookies, they were speckled with dark bumps and smelled a lot like the Ugly Mug.

Laz focused on loading our packs, stuffing them till all the pouches bulged.

Meteor yawned. 'We should sleep.'

'Don't be ignorant,' Laz told him. 'Gremlins sleep during the day. They're awake now.'

We hurried back to the coffee warehouse, lugging our packs.

At Laz's insistence, we wore the packs backwards, so the pouches were in front. He said it would make it easier to guard them. 'We'll see the little thieves coming, and we can fly away from them.'

But disaster awaited us. When we reached the portal back to Laz's café, we found it closed.

Laz flung himself at the warehouse wall several times, as if a new angle of approach would make a difference.

'Laz,' I said. 'Laz! The portal's gone.'

He stopped bashing himself against the concrete. 'Hobs and hooligans!' he swore. 'How can it be gone? I've kept it refreshed!'

'Someone sealed it,' Meteor answered.

'The location of this portal was known to exactly three.' Laz pointed to himself first, then moved his finger towards Meteor, then to me, where he stopped.

'You suspect *me*?' I asked.

'If not you, then who was it?' Were those *tears* slithering down his face?

'I want to get back to Feyland as much as you do.' How could I prove I'd had nothing to do with this? 'I'll open the portal again,' I offered, 'but only if you—'

'No!' he shouted. 'I don't want it back. I could never pass through that portal again without wondering who was lurking on the other side.'

'Maybe,' Meteor said, 'when you thought there was a spy, you were right.'

'Lily,' I said softly.

But Laz disagreed. 'Not her. If *she* found my portal, she'd bide her time.' He slammed his hand against the unyielding wall. 'Well, my fine young ones, we need to get out of here. And since the portals in the Golden Station are closed . . .'

He let the sentence hang. I knew what he meant: it was now up to me to get us home.

'Didn't you open another portal, the one close to Pix—' Meteor stopped as I shoved him.

Laz gathered his frayed robe closer. 'Shh. There could be spies listening.'

'You think we're being watched *now*?' I checked my pocket for the hundredth time. The vial of comet dust was still there, and so was the small bottle of aevum derk.

'Very possibly. And whoever it is can hide from a reveal spell,' Laz answered. 'Take us to your portal, Zaria.'

But I couldn't do that.

153

I didn't want Laz knowing any more of my secrets, especially the secret of my fondness for Sam. As Sam's genie godfather, Laz knew where he lived – but he would never guess on his own that Sam's basement housed a portal. I suspected the only thing Laz had ever done for Sam was to leave him alone. Certainly, I wouldn't be the one to urge him to pay more attention to his godchild. Sam was better off without him.

And as for Meteor, well . . .

Meteor had been with me when Sam blundered into Feyland. It was Meteor who urged me to cast the forgetting spell on my human friend. And if Meteor knew I'd visited Sam again afterwards, what would he think?

No, I couldn't do it; couldn't reveal my new portal to these genies.

Blast! Once again, I had no real choice. We had to get back to Feyland, and the only way to do it was through a portal. Since I didn't want to risk Sam and his family, I'd have to create a new portal. Again. Another thousand radia.

I was about to do exactly what Lily wanted me to do: use up more magic. *At her present rate, in a few months Zaria will be powerless.*

'I'll transport us,' I said, 'but to a place without a portal. Once we're there, I'll open one to . . . where we're going.' Thinking of all the places I'd been on Earth, I wondered which would be safe. Where in this world had I been that Lily knew nothing about?

Fuming, I turned to Laz, hating to trust him with anything so important. 'You know Earth better than we do; you've made thousands of journeys. Think of a place that's remote, and take us there.'

Laz smirked. 'You would put yourself in my power?'

I smiled as if I felt no fear. 'A gamble.'

Meteor wasn't smiling as he took my hand. We stood together on the warehouse floor, facing Laz. 'Transport us,' I said.

Chapter Twenty-nine

GREMLINS, LIKE GNOMES, ARE IMPERVIOUS TO SPELLS. THEY HAVE A LITTLE MAGIC OF THEIR OWN — JUST ENOUGH TO PASS THROUGH PORTALS TO EARTH. HOWEVER, GREMLINS MUST HITCH THEMSELVES TO ANOTHER TRAVELLER TO GET THROUGH A PORTAL. THE MAJORITY OF GREMLINS NEVER FIND THEIR WAY TO EARTH, FOR FEY FOLK ARE GENERALLY UNWILLING TO PROVIDE THESE SCREECHING MISCHIEF-MAKERS WITH PASSPORTS TO THE HUMAN WORLD. THOSE GREMLINS WHO MANAGE TO GET THERE ARE NOT INCLINED TO RETURN. AMONG HUMANS, THERE ARE ENDLESS CHANCES TO CREATE MISCHIEF, FOR HUMAN–BUILT MACHINES ARE FILLED WITH CRUCIAL SMALL PARTS THAT GREMLINS TAKE DELIGHT IN BREAKING. IN ADDITION, THERE ARE PLENTY OF BISCUITS TO BE FOUND.

Orville Gold, genie historian of Feyland

Looking around, I wondered if Laz had done something heinously dangerous — such as sending us to another world.

The shadowy landscape was nothing but rock. A bright

full moon shone down on heaps of boulders, making them look like the bones of unknown beasts. Under the boulders lay nothing but great slabs of stone. A few scrubby plants grew out of crannies here and there.

'Where are we?' I asked.

Laz was beside us, his leprechaun cap slightly askew, looking just as he always did – tall, lanky, a little greasy. 'You two sweethearts plan to hold hands for the rest of this trip?'

Meteor and I let go of each other.

'Are you going to tell us where on Earth we are?' Meteor asked.

'The wilds of Utah,' Laz answered. 'Very remote region. No one comes here. Ever. It's the perfect place for a portal: you won't have to add a barrier for stray humans with Level Five magic of their own.'

He was right about the place being remote: it was completely deserted except for the three of us. Laz had done what I asked, and now it was time for my part. But first I would put more protection on the comet dust. We were heading into a land of nimble thieves; it would be worth the loss of a little more radia to prevent the comet dust from being stolen. My spells weren't supposed to work on gnomes, but they had worked anyway. I could only hope they'd work on gremlins too.

I hesitated at the thought of Laz watching me cast a spell. But he already knew I was a Feynere. The comet dust was more important than keeping my methods secret.

I infused my wand. 'No one and nothing can steal the comet dust from me. Ever.'

Laz's wide grin made me uneasy. 'What an honour to see a Feynere in action. Even more of an honour to be told you carry comet dust!'

'You'd better keep that a secret,' Meteor said angrily.

'Of course.' Laz spread his hands, his grey-blue skin glowing oddly in the moonlight. 'And speaking of secrets, I've got some advice: aside from me, tell no one what you're doing, where you're going, or why. Especially gremlins. They keep no secrets: what one knows, they all soon know.' He wagged a finger at me. 'Guard yourself. Gremlins have no code of honour.'

'Unlike smugglers,' Meteor sniped.

Laz ignored him. 'They're pesky thieves, Zaria, and quite impervious to magic. Your precious spell won't hold them off.'

Meteor met my eyes. He must have heard my thought, because he said nothing about the way my magic had turned back gnomes.

'Enough talk,' I said, and thought of Leona. How were she and Andalonus faring among the pixies?

I flitted over to an extra-large boulder. It would make a good spot to open a portal. 'Take your bearings,' I told Laz. 'This will be the new portal. It will lead into gremlin territory.'

I spat on the boulder.

* * *

Part of the scene from Earth seemed to have followed us into the land of the gremlins. When we stepped through the Utah Portal, the first thing I saw was a pile of moonlit boulders. But these were in the middle of a field full of prickly, stinging plants that poked my ankles.

I floated up onto one of the biggest boulders and peeked over its top. Below me, hundreds of lanterns added their light to that of the moon and stars, showing a horde of gremlins.

Meteor joined me, squinting at the scene.

'They're not gruesome,' I whispered.

We'd been told that gremlins were covered with warts; that they were stunted creatures with sunken chests and arms so long their hands dragged along the ground. Their ears were supposed to be mere nubs on their misshapen skulls. But the gremlins hurrying along pebbled walkways under lanterns were only slightly shorter than fairies and genies. Between the bright moon and strong lantern light, I could see them well. Their arms were rather long; so were their fingers, but their hands did not drag on the ground. I saw no warts. Their neat ears, of normal size, were on rounded heads. They had oval eyes.

Unlike fairies and genies, these gremlins were all one colour – both their hair and skin was greenish-yellow. The males wore their hair in a short thick fuzz, the females in braids winding around their heads and tied up with flouncy ribbons. Simple clothes, no shoes. They had quick movements. When they ran, they dashed so fast they became a blur, yet never bumped into each other.

Gremlins, I'd been taught, were prone to shrieking, their shrieks so piercing they'd hurt the ears of anyone except other gremlins. Beryl had spoken of this as an established fact. But I heard no shrieks, none at all.

'Why aren't they shrieking?' I whispered to Laz, who hovered nearby.

'They don't shriek unless they're agitated.'

'There's nothing broken,' I said, surprised to find a gremlin village in working order. I couldn't see into any of the dwellings, but outside, the lanterns were well-trimmed, the pebbles on the walkways evenly spread, and everything clean. Hadn't I been told that gremlins broke anything they touched?

Laz grunted. 'Must be in the midst of a truce with the next village.'

'Truce?' Meteor hissed. 'You said they had no honour.'

'They don't.'

'They seem to be clever builders,' Meteor said.

'Of course they're clever – how else would they know how to break things?'

'But what are they doing now?' I asked, amazed by the numbers headed in the same direction. 'Where are they going?'

'The square,' Laz answered, pointing. 'They're gathering.'

I rose above the boulder to see better. From that height, I saw streams of gremlins converging into a crowd in front of one of the bigger buildings.

Laz and Meteor floated up to join me. 'We should go to a different village,' Laz muttered. 'There's another nest of grem—'

'Wait!' I cut him off. 'What if they're planning something? Don't you want to hear about it?'

Meteor nodded, but Laz sniffed. 'Gremlins in a crowd are not to be trifled with. We should go.'

But I wasn't willing to leave. These creatures fascinated me, especially because they were so unlike everything I'd been led to believe. 'I want to listen. It could be our chance to understand them.'

'Not safe.'

'They can't fly. If they run at us, we'll flee into the air.' Stubbornly, I watched as gremlins packed the open space, more arriving every second.

On one side of the square, a lone gremlin stood on a block of stone. He wore a heavy amber jewel around his neck that caught the lantern light. His bulbous little nose quivered as he waited for everyone to assemble. Finally he raised both long-fingered hands and cleared his throat. It sounded like a rusty bugle. All the gremlins quit shuffling their feet to stare up at him.

'Gremlins of Burdecka!' His voice was loud and blaring. 'I have received a message filled with rumours,' he trumpeted. 'I warn you, friends! Do not be misled by the new fey leader.'

New fey leader? Suddenly I was more awake.

He rolled on. 'Her promises are as empty as the biscuit packets of yesterday. She pretends she will have the power to make gremlins the magical equal of the greatest fairies and genies. She lies.'

Oberon's Crown! *Lily!* Lily Morganite must be calling herself the new leader of the fey! A terrifying idea pushed itself into my mind: with the durable spells breaking down all over Feyland, Lily Morganite might actually *be* the new leader. And apparently she was still promising to hand out magic — not only to her followers, but also to outlanders like gremlins. How far would she go for the chance to create aevia ray? And did she know, yet, that the comet dust had been taken?

I desperately hoped the councillors had gone to Anshield Island to tell the king and queen how badly the High Council had bungled. When they named Lily Morganite the Forcier of Feyland, they had brought on disaster and the theft of billions of radia. But would they admit what they had done?

We needed the help of our rightful rulers!

Chapter Thirty

In Feyland there is a group of islands in the middle of Glendonite Lake where days and hours do not behave the way they normally do. These islands are under an enchantment that changes the parameters of time. Anshield, the most famous of the archipelago, is the abode of King Oberon and Queen Velleron (also known as Mab). Their palace is surrounded by a sapphire wall woven with intricate spells that will not allow anyone to fly above it and prevents transport in or out.

No one has access to the sapphire stronghold without permission from the royal rulers.

Orville Gold, genie historian of Feyland

All the gremlins were gathered in the square to listen as their leader blared on – except the children, who played in the fields nearby. I moved away from the pile of boulders towards the children, creeping into one of the darker patches of shadow to sit on some softer ground and fold my tired wings.

The gremlin children fascinated me. The games they were playing involved running and jumping faster and faster till I couldn't tell one blur from another. Not far from me, one of them stood watching for a while before trying to join in. But when he darted in, bigger children tossed him off to the side. The limber little fellow somersaulted head over heels, then bounced up to try again. As I watched, he tried over and over but each time he was cast out. I wondered what kept him going back, and why they wouldn't let him be part of their fun. He fell and rolled so many times, I nicknamed him 'Tumble' to myself. If he kept it up, he was going to get hurt.

Again, someone picked him up and threw him with spiteful force. Tumble bunched himself into a ball as he hit the ground hard. He rolled right towards me. I reached out and caught him, holding him gently for a moment before setting him on his feet. He stared at me curiously as I opened my pack. Bringing out a large chocolate chip cookie, I gave it to him and saw a smile of wonder light up his face.

The gremlin leader's voice grew even louder: 'The fey leader *promises* to give an endless supply of biscuits to any one of us who will freely give her what is left of our stash, but—'

He never finished the sentence.

The adult gremlins began shrieking. The noise was so loud and piercing, it was like slivers of iron driving into my head. I clapped my hands over my ears.

Gremlin screeches were even worse than I'd been taught. And while I tried to shut out the hideous sound, a cluster of greedy eyes and hands crashed into me. Adult gremlins! One of them must have seen the cookie I'd given Tumble, and now it seemed the entire village was crowding up against me. Looking in concern for the little gremlin, I didn't see him anywhere. But it took the adults only seconds to strip off my pack, open it, and take the biscuits.

I tried to pick myself up, but gremlins were wedged around me so tightly I couldn't move, much less spread my wings. They chittered, 'Gimme gimme gimme,' their questing fingers searching for more biscuits even as they shoved the ones they had into their mouths.

Laz had told me to guard myself. I should have listened.

Screeches tore my ears, scrabbling fingers dug into my gown, the press of bodies robbed me of air.

As I struggled to breathe, I felt the deep Feynere power within me waking up. Overwhelming strength just beneath my skin threatened to toss the entire group of gremlin thieves into the sky. I didn't think about the radia I would lose, didn't think about anything at all except the need to take my next breath.

Then I heard Meteor's magically amplified voice boom out: 'Gremlins. Release the fairy and we will drop two more packs of biscuits.'

But it was too late. I couldn't hold onto the Feynere force. It burst from me in waves, throwing off the gremlins who were crushing me. They hurtled out from where I lay like seeds blown from a pod.

Spreading my sore wings, I flapped upward like a four-year-old learning to fly. Meteor zoomed towards me and supported me higher while I gasped for air. I felt so weak and depleted I couldn't even hover.

'Zaria?' His eyes were wary as he held me up.

'Oh, Meteor. I should have known you'd help; I should have waited. I . . . it happened again.' Fearfully I looked below, afraid I would see bodies. But although there was a clear spot where I had been attacked, all the gremlins were picking themselves up. The only effect of my blast of magic was to get them to quit screeching. The crowd had gone silent, hands stretched upward, fingers waving at the sky.

'Dastardly hobs!' Laz said beside us. 'They want more biscuits.' He shook his head, then turned his anger on me. 'What possessed you to offer a biscuit to a *gremlin on the ground*?'

I clung to Meteor. 'He was just a child,' I said. 'And the others were—'

'A child!' Laz sneered. 'Of course. And how much radia did it cost you to . . . do whatever you did?'

Strength. Give me strength! But I felt none. And I wasn't about to check my crystal watch while Laz was watching.

The smuggler shook his head disgustedly. 'These gremlins are in a full-blown frenzy, and they won't have their wits back for a while.'

166

'I'm sorry,' I said, feeling foolish and defeated.

Laz shrugged. 'The frenzy would have happened even without you, Zaria. All you did was make it worse. The Morganite's blasted message about unlimited biscuits will turn every gremlin village into a shambles.' He looked accusingly at Meteor. 'Someone must have helped her work out what the gremlin treasure is.'

'No scholar would help her,' Meteor said, his tone hostile.

'Keep your illusions if you like.' Laz pointed at the ground. 'But at any rate, we may as well move ahead to our next stopping point – among the trolls.'

'The trolls! Why not another gremlin village?' I asked. 'You and Meteor still have biscuits.'

He waved at the mob. 'Can't you see, every village will be like this one. By now, the Morganite will have delivered her message to all of them.'

'But without the gremlin biscuit, we can't make aevia ray,' I said. I didn't want to venture into Troll Country. We didn't have any plans for how to find the Nectara elixir. Not that our plans seemed to work out even when we had them.

I thought again of Leona and Andalonus. What if Lily had done something to disturb Pixandelle too?

'They'll begin shrieking again in another moment,' Laz said.

Meteor was looking at me, eyebrows up. 'I'll go if you

will.' His arm around me was about the only thing good in my life.

Staring at the ground, I decided that gremlins were ugly after all. What would be worse, going deaf, or going into Troll Country?

I nodded exhaustedly. 'We'll get the biscuit another time.'

'Can you fly?' Meteor asked.

'Probably,' I answered. 'If you hold my hand.'

'Touching,' Laz said.

But without help, I really wouldn't be able to fly any distance. Tremors shook my wings, and deep in my bones I felt hollow and used up.

'How far to Troll Country?' Meteor asked Laz. 'Can we transport?'

'No.' Laz turned and flew west. He seemed to have no doubt that we would follow.

When the gremlins saw us heading away without giving them any more biscuits, they began shrieking again. Clutching each other, Meteor and I started after Laz with no grace at all, off balance, tilting through the dark. Laz was only a blot zooming ahead of us, his cap pulled over his ears.

The gremlins streaked along below, running to keep up but gradually losing ground until their shrieks faded away. Squinting to see in the moonlight, we followed Laz over hills and valleys. Meteor had to do most of the flying for both of us. Soon, he shifted the biscuit pack around to his back and simply carried me in his arms. I was too tired to protest.

How much radia had I lost? I feared to find out but couldn't bear not knowing. After agonizing for a while, I decided to check my watch. Making sure that Laz was still far ahead of us, I flipped up the cover. I had to bring it close to my face to see. At first I thought the moonlight must be showing me the wrong mark.

'It isn't true,' I said.

'Zaria?' Meteor murmured. 'What isn't true?'

'It says I've spent another half-million radia. But all I did was throw some greedy gremlins off me!' I held up my watch so he could see.

Meteor's arms tightened around me. 'I'm sorry.'

It was true then. I was half a million radia poorer, with nothing to show for it, not even a biscuit from a gremlin. I hadn't needed my Feynere powers to save my life: if I'd waited one moment longer, Meteor would have made the mob let go of me.

What good was it to be a Feynere if my special magic could be so easily lost? At this rate, just as Lily had predicted, all my radia would soon be gone. Looking for comfort, I hid my face against Meteor's chest and focused on listening to him breathe.

I had to be more careful. More thoughtful. More like Meteor.

We were touching down, landing in a squishy field.

Meteor set me on my feet gently. Plants grew thickly all around us. They resembled grass, but their stalks were puffy. And slimy.

'Laz!' Meteor said. 'Why did you lead us into a swamp?'

'A little putch won't hurt you.' Laz adjusted his cap.

'This is putch? Trolls eat this?'

'Putch is their sonnia, you fool.'

Oh, how tired I was. Exhaustion beyond exhaustion. And a fog was rising.

Chapter Thirty-one

TROLLS ARE SAID TO HAVE A REMARKABLE SENSE OF SMELL, BUT THIS HAS NEVER BEEN VERIFIED BY A REPUTABLE SOURCE — PERHAPS BECAUSE REPUTABLE FEY FOLK AVOID TRAVELLING THROUGH TROLL COUNTRY.

TROLL FEMALES ARE ADEPT AT KEEPING THEMSELVES HIDDEN IF THEY WISH TO REMAIN UNSEEN. THEY CAN BLEND INTO THE LANDSCAPE ON TIRFEYNE AS IF THEY WERE MADE OF ROCKS AND SHRUBS. ON EARTH, THEY CAN APPEAR TO BE TREES. THEIR MAGIC IS QUITE AS POWERFUL AS THAT OF MALE TROLLS, BUT THEY ARE MORE LIKELY TO MAKE USE OF IT IN SECRET.

Orville Gold, genie historian of Feyland

I was awake and yet asleep. Or was I asleep and yet awake? I couldn't seem to move, but I heard rumbling voices.

'*It's her, I tell you.*'

'*Can't be. Fairies never come here.*'

'*She matches the description. And you can smell the difference.*'

Why couldn't I move?

'*You may be right. The young genie smells like a normal Blue.*

And there is a Yellow nearby who has an odour of trouble. But the fairy's scent . . .'

'It can be no one else. We must take her to King Ozriel.'

'What about her companions?'

'We'll bring the Blue.'

'And the other?'

'Leave him.'

My cheek rested on someone's shoulder, a shoulder that rolled and dipped with each step. I could hear the quiet of the night, broken by footfalls; I could feel the arms that held me. Yes, I was awake, but my eyes stayed closed, however much I willed them to open.

I tried to remember where I'd been before this long walk. There had been something I had meant to do, something that would help me and many others, something of great importance. But my mind felt slippery. I couldn't hold onto my own thoughts. *Enchanted. I'm enchanted.*

If I could just touch my wand! Was it still in the pocket of my gown? And wasn't there something else I carried – something just as important? I must be mistaken. If I had carried something as important as my wand, I would remember.

Where are we going?

I woke – if it can be called waking – when the one carrying me set me on my feet. Steadying hands kept me upright as

I found my balance. My eyes could finally open. At first, I saw only a haze. I kept blinking, and finally the haze cleared. What I saw jolted me. I was in a massive room. Gigantic blocks of stone, each bigger than any home in Galena, were stacked together to form walls fifty wingspans high. The stones had been fitted together so precisely no mortar was needed. The floor on which I stood shone as if polished, and soft light flooded the hall, though I couldn't tell where it came from.

And I was by no means alone.

The walls held rows and rows of balconies, filled with creatures looking quietly down on me, creatures unlike any I'd seen before.

Beside me, someone spoke. 'Trolls.'

I turned to my left and saw Meteor. He too was on his feet, propped by a large set of hands.

Trolls! We had studied them in school. But the descriptions we'd heard had been just as wrong as that of gremlins. First, we'd been told that trolls were bumbling and graceless. False. I knew that much already. The creatures who had carried Meteor and me had moved with an agile rhythm, never stumbling. Second, trolls were supposed to be twice the size of the tallest genie and immensely strong – able to crush rocks easily. But the trolls beside us were maybe a head taller than Meteor. Whether they could crush rocks, I didn't know. Third, trolls were said to be covered with thick pelts and have hideous faces. But this gathering of trolls had smooth skin in tones of orange, yellow and brown. Every one of them was dressed the same – in a simple brown tunic. Their wide-set eyes were big, black, and rather beautiful. They had broad mouths, thin lips and huge noses.

Not horrible. Just terrifying.

I tried to move my wings, but they hung like useless rags. And when I tried again to remember what I'd been doing right before the trolls found me, it was as if those memories had been drowned in dark water.

Surprisingly, I was able to slide my hand into my pocket to grip my wand. Why hadn't they taken it? They must not fear my magic in the least.

But I feared theirs.

The trolls in front of us were moving aside, clearing the area around a granite chair that was cut so smoothly it seemed to grow out of the floor. On it sat a troll whose skin had a golden gloss. His tunic was red rather than brown, with a border of bright yellow. He must be the king, for he wore a gleaming crown of carved wood.

So, trolls must also visit Earth, for on the world of Tirfeyne there was nothing from which to make a wooden crown. How frightening, to be a human unlucky enough to meet a troll.

I reached for Meteor's hand at the same moment he reached for mine. The scent of sonnia flowers suddenly filled the air, and I realized I was famished. A troll held a stone bowl next to my nose, a bowl filled with dried sonnia.

'Eat,' the king invited us. 'Refresh yourselves.' His rich voice filled the hall.

I took a handful of petals and stuffed them in my mouth. Meteor did the same. And though I hated being watched by thousands of trolls while we ate, the sonnia was excellent.

The troll king spoke. 'Sonnia from the times of yore.'

Puzzled, I glanced at Meteor, who bowed. I followed his lead, murmuring my thanks.

When I looked at the king, his eyes drew me in, and when I tried to look away, I could not.

His gaze was bringing back my memories! First, I recalled flying away from the gremlins. Then the trip to Earth with Laz. *Laz*. Where was he now? I remembered my own journey to Earth, remembered my theft of the comet dust – and why I had done it.

Aevia ray.

I let go of Meteor and thrust my hand in my pocket. The precious vial of dust was still there, along with the small bottle of aevum derk.

'Zaria Tourmaline.' It was the king speaking.

How did he know my name? Those who had carried me here had never spoken to me. They had talked only to each other. *It's her. She matches the description*. What description? And who had given it?

'You carry something of grave importance with you,' the king went on.

He knew about the comet dust? I didn't recall any search.

Were trolls able to walk through the minds of the fey? Did they know everything we knew and felt and dreamed? Maybe our minds were like scrolls to them, easy to read and easy to write on.

They had taken over my memories, taken away my ability to fly. At this moment, I could remember what I meant to do only because the king of the trolls had allowed it. Without so much as a wand, without a spoken spell, he could take that knowledge back again. He could make me forget everything, including my quest for aevia ray, my family, my dear friends.

No! I had to fight him.

The deep Feynere magic rose inside me, and I didn't try to stop it. But this time, something went wrong with my powers.

Chapter Thirty-two

Trolls are extravagantly rich in magic, and very secretive about their methods. No member of the fey has succeeded in discerning how troll magic is done, but evidently, trolls can easily adapt their spells to cling to objects. Their magic also has an affinity for liquid, making it well-suited to enchantments that are dissolved into beverages.

Sometimes the effects of troll magic are fleeting, sometimes the effects are lasting, but always the effects are powerful.

Orville Gold, genie historian of Feyland

Terrifying silence, absence of all sound. Nothing in my vision; it was as if my eyes were gone. I couldn't sense my wings, couldn't even tell if my heart was still beating. I stood in the midst of nothingness that went on and on.

The only thing I knew was that my power was draining away.

Stop!

But I didn't know how.

I heard my name. It landed inside the void like a

butterfly fluttering in a storm: weak and faint, stunned by forces much bigger and stronger than it could ever be.

'Zaria.' A little louder.

Who was calling? I knew that voice, knew it was dear to me.

Pressure on my hand, squeezing hard, hard enough to push against the nothingness. I wanted to squeeze back, but my fingers wouldn't move.

'Zaria!'

The pressure moved to my shoulder, then to both shoulders, fastening like clamps. Shaking me. Shaking away the void.

Life rushed back.

I could see again — see Meteor's face, his emerald eyes. No sight had ever been more welcome.

Quivering with weakness, I heard the voice of the troll king.

'Your powers mean nothing in the palace of the trolls,' he said.

Why? Hadn't I taken on troll magic before when I turned their cloak to aevum derk? But that had not been in the palace of the trolls or in the presence of this king.

At least he had released his hold on my vision.

He spoke again. 'We will not take your comet dust from you, Zaria Tourmaline.'

Astounding.

'You won't?' I blurted out.

'We trolls do not interfere with trivial squabbles among the fey,' he answered.

The comet dust was just a trivial squabble to him?

'And besides,' he continued, 'this is no trivial battle you fight.'

I was having great trouble keeping upright, and feeling wretchedly confused.

The King of the Trolls rumbled on. 'The outcome will determine whether fey magic will endure or sink into nothingness. As your neighbours, we take an interest in a matter so central to the world of Tirfeyne.'

As our neighbours? I wondered if the trolls had any idea of their reputation among the fey. We thought of them as dangerous monsters to be avoided – and for good reason.

'We will give you the Nectara elixir you seek,' the king rumbled. 'But you must promise that if you succeed in making aevia ray, you will give it all to your king and queen.'

I gulped. He knew about aevia ray. 'Y-you'll *give us* Nectara elixir?'

'I will give it to *you*, Zaria Tourmaline. Only because you are one of the Feynere.'

He knew that too.

'Give us your promise,' he said.

I held onto Meteor and stared at the shining floor. How could I make such a promise? A young fairy like me would never be allowed entrance to the sapphire stronghold. Did the troll king expect me to break down the gates? For I would not trust a councillor to deliver aevia ray.

If you succeed, he had said.

Aevia ray could not be made without Nectara elixir. And stealing Nectara would be impossible, I knew that now. We could never slip past the troll guards, and overpowering them was out of the question.

Without Nectara elixir, no aevia ray. Without aevia ray, Lily Morganite would keep taking over Feyland. There would be no one to stop her unless King Oberon and Queen Velleron had enough radia to fight her. They would need aevia ray to help them, not only to win such a battle but also to repair the durable spells.

'Your promise,' the king said again, his voice colder now.

If I wanted the Nectara, I would have to agree.

'Yes,' I said. 'If we succeed in making aevia ray, I will give it to the king and queen of the fey.' Somehow, I would find a way into the sapphire stronghold.

'YOUR PROMISE,' the crowd shouted, and the stones beneath me shook with the vibration of their voices. The hall seemed smaller suddenly, and the trolls larger.

Fear spread across my wings. 'I promise.'

The king raised a solemn hand. 'We will hold you to it.'

'WE WILL HOLD YOU TO YOUR WORD.' From the balconies, thousands of black eyes looked down on me.

Then silence began building, and I felt an overwhelming sense of menace. Had I done something wrong?

Meteor whispered out of the corner of his mouth. '*Offer him something.*'

Of course. Meteor, the councillor's son, knew protocol. I must offer the king a gift to show my gratitude for the Nectara elixir. Something of value.

I tried to think of the words Meteor would use. 'Uh,' I began. 'Your Highness, in gratitude, I wish to present you with a gift. The comet dust I carry is the most precious thing I have. Would you accept a portion of it for the trolls?'

'An honourable offer, Zaria Tourmaline,' the king answered. 'But trolls have no use for comet dust.'

'Then,' I quavered, 'what might I give that you would find worthy?'

The king touched his crown. 'A portion of the aevum derk.'

He knew about the aevum derk.

Did that explain why the trolls had brought me to their king? My mind raced and stumbled. Why would the trolls want aevum derk?

I didn't want to give up the little I had left. It was my fall-back, my last resort, my mighty weapon against Lily Morganite.

While I agonized, I felt the menace in the hall again, as if everyone there had drawn an iron club.

'I carry a small amount of aevum derk,' I said. 'I will give it to you.'

The king inclined his head as if he were doing me a

favour instead of the other way around. 'We thank you, Zaria Tourmaline.'

Digging in the pocket of my gown, I brought out the small bottle I'd taken from Sam's room. Sam! I wished I had something else belonging to him. Even a button from a shirt he had worn would be better than nothing.

Not knowing the protocol, I tottered forward. I would have flown, but my wings would not lift me. Bowing in front of the king, I offered him the bottle.

He took it from me. Seized it. And opened it.

He opened my Feynere seal! It took him no effort. None. Then he brought the bottle to his large nose and sniffed. Triumphant glee shone in his eyes while I stood with clasped hands.

'Zaria Tourmaline,' the king boomed. 'We wish you well on your journey. May you achieve your quest.'

'Thank you.' I strove to conceal how wretched I felt. With the aevum derk gone, every hope for defeating Lily lay in creating aevia ray.

'You will now be escorted to the borders.' He rose abruptly, towering over me.

But where was the Nectara elixir? I had just given the troll king the last of the aevum derk. Had this whole ritual been nothing more than a ploy to get me to give it away? What if the trolls had need of aevum derk freely given from a fairy?

If so, I had fallen straight into their trap.

The king bowed ever so slightly. 'One wish, Zaria Tourmaline.'

This time, there was no echo from the great gathering. Instead, a gasp swept the hall and gusted over me.

Without understanding what was happening, I found myself gazing at polished wooden beads strung on the necklace the king wore. Then he laid his hand on my head, and hot light seared through me in painful bursts. I would have jumped away if there had been any strength in my wings or legs.

He withdrew his hand. Spots stabbed my eyes. Tears ran down my face as I tried to expand my useless wings, tried to see around me.

Chapter Thirty-three

EVERY LAND HAS ITS CUSTOMS. THE WISE TRAVELLER WILL LEARN AS MUCH AS POSSIBLE ABOUT THEM BEFORE ARRIVING IN AN UNKNOWN PLACE.

Orville Gold, genie historian of Feyland

When my eyesight returned, the king was gone. So were all the other trolls except two – those who had brought us to this place.

The troll beside me had livid orange skin, and I wondered why I hadn't noticed his colour earlier. The one next to Meteor was pale yellow.

'The fey must be as inane as history proclaims,' said the yellow one. 'The king himself bestows the one wish upon a *fairy*, and she behaves as if she has been harmed. He agrees to give Nectara elixir to a *fairy*, and she does nothing but weep.'

The orange troll took a step forward and bent to peer in my face. 'The one wish has never before been given to one of the fey,' he said.

'One wish?' I asked faintly. I wanted so badly to leave here. To fly. What had they done to my wings? Would I ever take to the skies again?

'His Majesty gave you a wish, Zaria Tourmaline. A true wish, at a time of your choosing, certainly granted,' the troll answered, straightening up.

He can do that? I thought about using the wish immediately, wishing to fly. I'd soar away and take Meteor with me.

'It is a great honour,' the troll told me coldly.

'This wish,' Meteor said. 'Please tell us how it can be used?'

The orange troll spoke. 'It must be a wish of your heart, fairy – a wish spoken aloud. It cannot be ordered by another unless you agree.' Bending close to me again, his face was sombre. '*One* wish, and one only.'

A wish of my choosing, *certainly granted*. This was magic greater than my own. How often had I dreamed of what I would do if I could have any wish? I'd wish for my family to be with me.

The yellow troll broke in, his voice harsh. 'Some things are forbidden, Zaria Tourmaline. Your wish cannot pass through portals or cross worlds, and it cannot bring back the dead.'

I looked at him, fear running through my wings. How many of my innermost thoughts could he read? Or was he telling me my family was dead?

I must decide carefully which words would bring my family to me. If they lived.

But the troll was still talking. 'You can use your wish in

any land of Tirfeyne except one.' Black eyes stared me down. 'Troll Country,' he said. 'Do you understand?'

I fought back from the dream of reuniting with my family, back to where I was – in the palace of the trolls.

'Yes,' I answered bleakly. 'I understand.'

Would they let us go now? Although Meteor and I had left Feyland only the night before, it seemed a long time since we'd been home. I felt I would fade like a wilted sonnia flower if I didn't get back there soon – if I didn't see the rooftops glinting like medallions, didn't see the fey skies glowing, or the great Gateway to Galena arching high and wide. I needed to be there, even though the gateway's magic was gone and the skies had darkened and the portals were closed.

'We will escort you to the border.' The orange troll calmly lifted me.

I tried to keep my dignity. 'We could transport, and save you the trip.'

The troll began walking. 'You overestimate your powers.'

Before I could reply or look round for Meteor, a thick mist covered my mind.

Troll magic.

They brought us to the spot from which they'd taken us – the place at the edges of gremlin territory. They removed the blurry haze they'd placed over our minds and set us on our feet. I didn't know how it was done; I heard no spells, saw no gestures or wands.

Daylight showed we were on the edge of an enormous swampland filled with putch. It stretched into the distance like a squishy lake.

The orange troll handed me a small, plain sack tied with string. I could feel the shape of a slender jar inside it.

'Nectara,' he said. 'Do not lose it.'

The yellow troll thrust a larger sack into my free hand. 'Dried sonnia. By order of the king.'

I wavered, my wings gummy and limp, my legs wobbly. Ignoring me, the trolls turned and left. I watched them walk away with their smooth, rolling gait.

Carefully I set down the sonnia to stash the Nectara in my pocket where the aevum derk had been. Slowly I picked up the sonnia and held it in both hands. 'Why would the trolls give us food?'

'I don't know,' Meteor said. 'But they took my biscuits.'

It was true; the human-made backpack he'd been wearing when we entered Troll Country was missing now.

I tried to stuff the sack of sonnia into one of my pockets, but it was too large. Meteor offered to carry it, and it fitted easily into a pocket of his robe. Then he tested his ability to fly but couldn't lift off the ground; all he could manage was short, awkward hops. I tried my wings, but they wouldn't unfurl.

'Troll magic,' Meteor said. 'Worse than anything.'

'Much worse,' I agreed.

'Being in that palace was like wearing iron boots on my feet and an iron helmet on my head.'

'They can walk through the hallways of our minds, can't they?' I said. 'That's how they knew all about me.'

Meteor nodded glumly. 'I didn't know that about them before – and I wish I didn't know it now. I hope this visit to Troll Country doesn't mean they can invade our thoughts at whim from now on.'

I hoped not too. 'Meteor, I didn't thank you. If it hadn't been for you, I would have used every last bit of my radia trying to fight the king. Thank you.'

'Of course. Zaria, I would—'

'My Feynere magic had no effect on the trolls. None! And I don't dare check my watch to see how much I lost.' I held up my wrist. 'Will you?'

Meteor's touch was gentle as he circled my wrist with a hand and then opened the cover on my crystal watch. He looked, then pressed his lips together as he closed it again. 'I'm sorry.'

'How much?' I whispered.

Swallowing, he looked at me miserably. 'Another five million.'

Heedless of the slimy putch, I sank to the ground. A few weeks ago, I had registered full Violet. Ten million radia, a fortune by any measure. And now, there was less than three and a half million of that left.

Meteor sat in the squelching putch at my side and did

his best to console me. He reminded me that we had gained the Nectara elixir, something that had seemed impossible. We were free to leave Troll Country, something that he had feared would never happen. And we needed to get back to Feyland, where Leona and Andalonus might be waiting for us.

Finally he scooped me into his arms and held me, telling me he would have done the same if he were a Feynere; that the magic of trolls scared him more than anything he had ever read or imagined; that he would have tried anything to get out of their enchantments.

'Really?' I asked. 'You would have done the same?'

'The very same.'

'I'm so tired, Meteor.'

'I'll help you. Let's at least get away from the border.'

A drizzly fog was rolling in, concealing the landscape as we turned towards gremlin territory. Still unable to fly, we were forced to walk. Meteor stomped ahead, thumping the ground to create a path for me. My skirts were coated with slime and clung to my legs, slowing me.

There was no marker as we left Troll Country, no magical alarm. But the plant-life changed from putch to thorny plants, and when we left the swamp, I heard Meteor give a big sigh. 'Look!' He rose enough to clear the stickers covering the ground. 'Try your wings again, Zaria.'

This time they opened. Finally I could fly, though not well. Meteor helped me, holding my hand as we flew on.

'Meteor, I want to use my wish,' I said.

'To find your family. I know.'

'You don't *know*.'

'Zaria, we've been friends since before your family . . .' His voice trailed off.

'They didn't die!'

'According to *Laz*, they didn't. But how many times has he lied to you?'

'If he's right and they're alive, I have to find out, don't I?'

Meteor turned in mid air and caught me by the shoulders. '*If.*'

'You think they're dead.'

'I hope they're alive.' His eyes were soft.

I thought it over again. 'Maybe *I* could wish to be wherever my family is, instead of wishing they were next to me.'

He shook his head. 'Whether you go to them or they come to you, if they're in glacier cloth, even your Feynere powers won't be enough to free them. Remember, only the one who casts the glacier spell can reverse it.'

I hated thinking what it would mean to *find* my family but be unable to free them. 'Maybe that isn't true. Maybe I wouldn't have to get Lily to agree.'

'And if it is true? Or what if you use the trolls' wish and it lands you in a trap?' He was frowning with worry. 'And what if your family's hidden somewhere on Earth? The trolls said your wish cannot cross worlds – so you would use it up for nothing.'

I looked at the desolate rocks and stickers below. 'One wish,' I said. 'If only the trolls had given me two.'

Meteor's hands tightened on my shoulders. 'Zaria, remember what the King of the Trolls said about why he would let you keep the comet dust? *The outcome will determine whether fey magic will endure or sink into nothingness.*' He lifted his eyebrows.

'You want me to use the wish for Feyland,' I said bitterly.

He nodded, letting me go. 'I'm so sorry, Zaria, but suppose what he said is true? There's no question that fey magic has been dwindling steadily for two hundred years. No one knows why – and no one wants to speak of it, not even members of the council – including my father.'

'Of course not,' I said even more bitterly. 'What have the councillors ever done to help Feyland?'

'So who will?'

Sighing, I looked back at the mist covering Troll Country. I should have asked the king more questions. *What do you mean, sink into nothingness? How much time do we have to save the magic? How do we get into the sapphire stronghold? What are your plans for the aevum derk?*

Too late for that now. I hoped it wasn't too late for everything else.

My eyes stung as if I'd rubbed them with prickers. 'All right. I don't have to use the wish right away. I'll wait.'

Meteor didn't say I was doing the right thing. He didn't say anything at all, and I could have kissed him for it.

'We have our magic back,' I said, taking his hand again. 'We should transport home.'

'Allow me. *Transera nos.*'

Chapter Thirty-four

FAIRIES AND GENIES HAVE ALWAYS BEEN FASCINATED BY TIME: WHAT IT IS AND HOW IT OPERATES. IT HAS BEEN SAID THAT SOME AMONG THE ANCIENTS MASTERED TIME TO SUCH AN EXTENT THAT THEY COULD STEP OUTSIDE OF IT AT WILL. THIS MAY BE TRUE, FOR HOW ELSE COULD THE SPELLS UPON ANSHIELD ISLAND BE EXPLAINED? AND SADLY, BY WHAT OTHER MEANS COULD THE GLACIER SPELL HAVE BEEN DEVISED?

Orville Gold, genie historian of Feyland

When we landed in my mother's room, I heard a horrendous noise, and saw Leona and Andalonus huddled on the floor with their hands over their ears.

'That sounds like gremlins!' I screamed.

Leona pointed to the window.

Meteor and I hurried to look out. The scene below showed pandemonium, worse than the day Lily had brought her gnomes. Much worse.

A great horde of gremlins was jumping up and down in front of my home, their long fingers outstretched, their mouths open so wide I could see down their throats. As I watched, a big group of them – adults and children both – threw themselves against my door. When they hit the magic barrier the house shivered and they fell back, shrieking piercingly. But as soon as they retreated, more gremlins attacked.

I clapped my hands over my ears to shut out their keening cries. The gremlins must believe I had more biscuits – but how had they found where I lived? I didn't think they had even noticed me – only the biscuits I carried.

Even more shocking, it wasn't only gremlins gathered outside. Above and behind them hovered fairies and genies, all covering their ears. When the gremlins quieted for an instant, I could hear angry shouts: 'Zaria! Help! Let us in!'

Many were fey folk I knew. Fairies and genies who had been my classmates. Their parents. Those who lived in Galena.

Another swell of screeches crashed the barrier. Impatiently I drew my wand. 'Block the sound from outside.'

The silence was a terrible relief.

Andalonus rose from the floor to hug me. 'You've saved my ears from death.'

'Thank you, Zaree,' Leona said. 'We were going mad.'

'What's going on?' I asked. 'Why are all those fey folk asking for help – from me?'

Leona answered. 'Gremlins have raided every other

home in Galena, breaking everything from clocks to stoves to toys from Earth. Who knows what they're doing in Oberon City. No one can stop them, they're everywhere. I tried using magic on them, even the statue spell. Nothing works. And yours is the only place free of them.'

'The only place? No.'

'Yes,' she went on. 'And that crowd out there is angry at me too, Zaree. They believe we Violet fairies should go around Feyland and repair the durable spells. When they saw me with Andalonus out in Galena, they charged me, screaming and crying.'

Andalonus nodded gloomily. 'True. They said you were hoarding your magic.'

Leona flicked her fingers at the window. 'I tried to tell them, Zaree – that we're only fourteen, and *we* didn't let the durable spells slip. *We* didn't steal the magic tax that was supposed to go to the durable spells. Lily Morganite did!'

Out of the window, close to the front of the crowd, I could see my old classmate Portia Peridot, her green wings fluttering. Next to her was Cora. I caught sight of Tuck Lodestone too, and others I knew. Some were with their parents, but not Tuck. Maybe, just maybe, Magistria Lodestone was off to Anshield Island to let the royals know about the chaos; maybe, just maybe, the rest of the council was there too.

'Please, Zaria,' Andalonus said. 'Let them in – the fairies and genies.'

'Have any of them tried to get through?' I asked. *Do any of them care about me?*

'They run into your shield.'

I rubbed my forehead with a tired hand. 'If I lift it, the gremlins will come in too – and everyone else who wants to harm us.' My friends watched as I turned my back on the window and collapsed into my mother's nest. 'I'd have to redo the whole enchantment. It used up tens of thousands of radia the first time.'

Andalonus twisted strands of his blue hair. 'You're watching out for your radia? At a time like this?'

'She's right.' Turning from the window, Meteor wore a heavy frown. 'There are hundreds of fairies and genies out there. How would she decide who gets to come in? They're all in a panic.' He looked at me. 'Save your magic, Zaria. The gremlins won't stay for ever.' He faced Andalonus. 'If those fey folk had any love for Zaria, they could open the door. It's not her fault.' He pulled the curtain shut.

Leona floated over to me. 'It's not that everyone hates you, Zaree. They haven't all tried the door.' She looked tired, I could see it now. As for Andalonus, he closed his eyes and sank onto the cushions of the window seat.

'Did you get the pixie song?' Meteor asked.

Nodding, Leona pointed at Andalonus. 'Would you believe yes?'

'You got the song!' I touched a wing to Leona's then

196

flew to hug Andalonus. 'Did you like dancing with the pixies?'

He groaned.

Leona explained. 'He had to do a lot of singing and dancing while I hid and spied on him. The pixies almost carried him away for ever, but we got out with the song.'

I smiled at Andalonus. 'My sympathies.'

'And what about you?' Leona asked. 'Did you get the gremlin biscuit?'

Meteor snorted. 'No,' he answered, floating back to the window. 'But we got the Nectara from the trolls.' He pulled a corner of the curtain and peeked out. 'Oberon's Crown!' he roared before Leona and Andalonus could react to our news. 'Your protection is failing, Zaree. Gremlins are getting past it.'

'What?' I darted to the window in time to see a mob of gremlins hurl themselves against the barrier. None got through. 'What do you mean?'

'I saw a gremlin run right inside,' he insisted.

'Are you sure?' Rushing to open the door, I listened at the landing, my friends crowding close behind.

We heard muffled clanking sounds and flew at high speed down to the hearth room.

A small gremlin was hunched in a corner holding my family clock. He'd already managed to open it, and his little hands were crammed inside its workings.

My family clock! I swooped in on the gremlin. How

dare he! I made a grab for the clock, but he scuttled away, leaving me holding nothing but air.

'Give that back!' I screeched so loudly I could have been a gremlin myself.

Meteor, Leona and Andalonus each tried to snatch the clock. Meteor almost nabbed the gremlin's shoulder, but no one else came anywhere near catching him.

'How did you get in?' Meteor yelled.

The creature leaped onto our lowest perch. All four of us converged on him. Squeezing the clock with both arms, he squeaked defiantly.

For the first time, I got a good look at his face. 'Tumble? Why are you breaking my clock?'

'Already broken,' he said in a piping voice. *Scamp!*

'Give it to me,' I ordered, extending my hand.

He hunched over it more closely. 'Why can't I fix it?'

'Fix it?' Meteor exclaimed.

'Gremlins don't fix things,' Leona said.

Tumble stuck out his lower lip. 'We know *how*,' he said. 'Not supposed to.'

What? I remembered how his fellow gremlins had booted him out of their game. Was he an outcast because he liked to *fix* things? 'All right, then,' I said. 'Fix the clock.'

Tucking his feet under him, he set to work. I watched as he adjusted tiny gears with his nimble fingers. Every now and then he held the clock to his ear. Soon, an extra-wide grin split his face. Bending close, I heard a soft, even ticking.

'You did it!' I hugged the little imp and joined him on the perch.

But just then, Laz strolled in.

Chapter Thirty-five

FAIRIES AND GENIES ARE ENJOINED TO USE THEIR MAGIC
WITH CARE, ALWAYS CONSIDERING, *BEFORE* CASTING A
SPELL, WHAT ITS EFFECTS MAY BE. FOR IT IS WELL KNOWN
THAT AN ENCHANTMENT OF BENEFIT TO ONE MAY WELL BE
THE DOWNFALL OF ANOTHER.

Orville Gold, genie historian of Feyland

Laz still wore his backpack turned frontways. 'Glad I could
join you,' he said caustically.

My friends were all staring at him, while his eyes moved
lazily from one to another of us. 'What? No words of
welcome?' he said. 'Only seek me out when you're in
trouble? Which, by the way, you're in now – if you haven't
noticed.'

'Oberon's Crown!' Leona whirled on me. 'The smuggler
loves you?'

Amazed, I gazed at the lanky genie. Did he love me? Laz?
Was it possible? But then my eyes went to the battered cap
on his head. 'Tell them about your cap, Laz,' I hurried to say,
afraid Leona had betrayed the secret of how my protections
worked.

'Yes, I have great fondness for Zaria,' he told Leona,

sneering. He wrinkled his nose. 'Is that putch I smell?'

Glancing at my skirts, I saw just how bedraggled and filthy they were. There was definitely a stench coming from me – and, now that I noticed, from Meteor too. I whipped out my wand. 'Clean clothes,' I muttered, waving in the direction of us both, relieved when my gown freshened and so did Meteor's robes. It was a wasteful use of magic, but at that moment saving time seemed more important.

'Your cap? Tell them,' I said to Laz, rising from the perch. Well, I tried to rise, but Tumble clung so tightly to my waist, I lost my balance and fell back onto the pillows. Gently, I unfastened his arms, putting the mended clock into his hands. Clutching it, he scooted back, almost disappearing in the worn cushions.

'Laz's cap is magic,' Meteor told Leona. 'It protects him from all enchantments.'

Laz bowed again, mockingly. Even when he bent far forward, the cap remained on his head. 'Including Feynere enchantments,' he said. 'And all it cost me was a hand of cards.'

Leona flew at the smuggler, grabbing the brim of his hat. She gave it a tug but it didn't move. She tugged harder. The hat stayed fixed to Laz's stringy hair.

He clicked his tongue. 'Careful, my temperamental fairy. This cap can only change hands voluntarily – much like one of the ingredients of aevia ray.'

Leona looked at me in disbelief. 'You told him about aevia ray?'

'He *guessed*.'

She brandished her wand at Laz. 'Give me that cap.'

The smuggler chuckled gratingly. 'No.'

Leona infused fully. Level 200 magic, twice as much as the highest-level fairies and genies in Feyland!

'Wait, Leona,' I cried.

Her eyes changed from silver to hard grey as she aimed her wand at Laz. '*Resvera den!*' The breaking spell – with more power behind it than anyone had ever used.

The cap should have fallen from Laz's head. Not only that, it should have been turned to dust. Instead, it transformed, changing from battered to jaunty. Even the shabby feather perked up.

Panting, Leona lowered her wand.

Laz grinned. 'Thank you, my lovely. You just gave me some of your power.' He swept her a bow.

'G-gave you power?' Leona sputtered.

'Absorbed by my cap.' Laz brushed his feather. 'A convenient feature, considering the company.'

A jolt shook the walls. I glowered at Laz. 'Did you use the front door? Everyone out there will think I've let you in on purpose.'

'Of course I didn't. I used a window on the first floor. As I told you before, Zaria, gremlins are pesky thieves.' He pointed a languid finger at Tumble. 'And although no doubt many in the crowd are angry that I got in when they couldn't, everyone saw *him* walk in. Trust me, gremlins are far more hated just now than I am.'

I turned to look at the little gremlin. He bounded up from his perch and raced across the room with the clock, setting it in its place on the mantel. While he was close to the hearth, I shivered with fear for his safety. What if Lily suddenly appeared there again?

I held out my hands to him, and he darted over and leaped into my arms. The little rascal was grinning and patting my face. *Only those who love me may enter this house as long as I'm alive.* I smiled fondly back at Tumble.

'Zaria?' Laz said. 'How did the gremlin get in?'

'How much is the answer worth to you?' I said spitefully. I didn't like the way his eyes slid from me to Tumble and back again.

Tumble wriggled, so I set him down. Something streaked between me and Laz, and I heard a crinkling sound. When Laz lunged for the gremlin at his feet, I leaped in the smuggler's way. He caught hold of my arm. I shook him off, trying my best to look dangerous.

Tumble appeared just out of reach, holding a paper sack with grease stains on its side. He pulled out a thick biscuit. 'Snicker doodle,' he burbled.

'I warned you, they're pesky thieves!' Laz made another grab for the gremlin.

'Biscuit for Zaree,' Tumble said, beaming, and offered it to me.

I gaped at him. We all did. Every one of us stood perfectly still, our mouths hanging open, Laz's the widest.

Finally Meteor nudged me, and I reached out. The little gremlin turned his hand over and dropped the biscuit into mine. 'Thank you,' I breathed. 'Thank you!' I carefully transferred the biscuit to Meteor before hugging Tumble. 'All the rest of our biscuits belong to you,' I told him.

'To me.' He grinned. 'And Zaree!' He held out another.

'You eat it,' I said, smiling.

He chomped down, cooing delightedly, sprinkling crumbs all over the dilapidated rug.

Chapter Thirty-six

To accomplish anything of greatness, it is often necessary to proceed without knowing what the outcome will be. History teaches us that the unexpected is filled with magic of its own, and not one of us can predict the events of our lives. All of us look back in wonder, perplexed and astonished by the events we have witnessed.

Orville Gold, genie historian of Feyland

I was so happy about Tumble's gift, even the sight of Laz still hovering in my circle of friends couldn't irritate me – at least not unbearably.

'We have all the ingredients except one?' I asked.

'You got the Nectara?' Laz seemed truly awestruck. 'But the trolls captured you!' His gravelly voice rose an octave. 'When I heard a rumour you'd escaped, I came straight here. How did you get away, let alone steal Nectara?'

'A rumour? Who could have told you?' Meteor was glaring at the smuggler. 'Did you even try to rescue us from the trolls?'

'Of course not,' Laz answered. 'I may be many things, my

fine young genie, but a fool is not one of them – and it would take a very great fool for that. Believe me, I was more than happy to be left behind when they took you away, though why they would capture such a small—' He stopped, and rubbed his face with his knuckles, looking grim. 'Feynere,' he said. 'They know, don't they?'

'Yes,' I answered.

'What did they want for the Nectara, Zaria?'

But I wasn't going to tell him.

'Tell me you didn't give aevum derk to the trolls.'

When I didn't answer, he nodded. 'So that's how you got away.' He looked completely different now: not lazy or care-less, not angry or amused. Instead, he looked tired. Very tired. He shook his head and yanked on his cap. 'Nothing to be done about it now.'

'Thank you,' Meteor said sarcastically. 'Without your wisdom, we would never have guessed that much.'

Laz gave him a baleful grin. 'One day, you'll seek my help but won't find it.'

I sighed, hoping to avoid a quarrel between them. 'Let's go up to the first storey and decide what to do about finding the thing cherished by leprechauns.' I hoped my friends would remember why my mother's room would be a safer place to talk about the last ingredient for aevia ray. The blackened ashes in the centre of the hearth should remind them.

'Yes,' Leona said. 'Laz can stay here and watch the gremlin.'

'Not likely.' Laz was himself again, his tone baiting, his cap tilted at an arrogant angle. 'You need me.'

'What for?' I asked.

'I have the final ingredient.'

'Of *course* you do,' Leona said scornfully.

'Upstairs,' I said. 'We'll discuss it there.' I didn't like the idea of Laz in my mother's room, but short of asking Meteor to jab him with the poker we'd never get rid of him.

Leona turned to lead the way. Tumble bounded over to me, shedding biscuit crumbs. He tugged on my arm, pointing to the highest perch. There lay Andalonus, sound asleep.

Of course. The aftermath of dancing with the pixies.

He was so groggy, it took both Meteor and Laz to get him off the perch. They carried him up to my mother's nest, where he sank into deep sleep again in an instant. Leona flopped down next to him, yawning.

'Don't worry,' she said before I could ask. 'I won't go to sleep. Yet.'

I took a quick peek outside. The crowd was just as large, but now it was mostly fey folk. The gremlins must have got tired of flinging themselves at an invisible wall, and left. Not so the fairies and genies. There were more of them now, watching the door with cold fury.

Chapter Thirty-seven

ON EARTH, THERE ARE SKILLED HUMAN SURGEONS WHO CAN MEND DIRE INJURIES. IN THIS REGARD, HUMANS HAVE FAR SURPASSED FEY MAGIC, FOR ON TIRFEYNE, HEALING SPELLS DO NOT EXIST.

AS CHILDREN, FAIRIES AND GENIES ARE CAREFULLY NURTURED IN GALENA SO THAT NO INJURY MAY BEFALL THEM. LAWS AGAINST HARMING ONE ANOTHER ARE STRICT, FOR THOUGH MINOR INJURIES WILL HEAL FOR US JUST AS THEY DO FOR HUMANS, WE HAVE NO ENCHANTMENTS THAT CAN MEND A BROKEN WING OR RESTORE A SIGHTLESS EYE.

THERE ARE ONLY TWO HEALERS IN FEYLAND: SONNIA FLOWERS AND TIME. SOMETIMES, NEITHER IS ENOUGH.

Orville Gold, genie historian of Feyland

Tumble curled up beside me on the window seat and fell asleep with a half-eaten ginger snap in his sticky fingers. His snores were much louder than I would have expected from someone so small, but they were somehow soothing.

'Lovely room,' Laz commented, leaning against a wall. 'Wonderful tile work.' He reached inside his genie robe with the air of a hero and pulled out a foil packet that had obviously been made on Earth. 'Something cherished by leprechauns. My best mocha, a blend of coffee and cocoa.' He tossed it to Meteor. 'I call it Le MoCo.'

Meteor caught the packet, but his eyebrows drew together. 'Coffee and cocoa? You think *this* is an ingredient for aevia ray?'

'Leprechauns will offer to scrub the floor with their beards for a chance at one sip of that brew. They cherish it.'

Meteor hurled the packet, and it struck the wall before smacking against the floor. 'The recipe for aevia ray goes back four thousand years! It's not going to list a combination of roasted beans *you* smuggled here from Earth last week.'

Laz scooped up the packet. 'Would you rather *guess* what leprechauns might have fancied four thousand years ago? If you know anything about enchantments, you should know they adapt to the situation at hand.'

'I'd rather not take your word for what leprechauns cherish,' Meteor answered.

Laz gave a conceited shrug. 'I have more experience with leprechauns than any genie alive.'

'More experience cheating them, lying to them, and tricking them,' I said, remembering Meechem handing over his cap.

'No one forces them to join my games.'

Leona rose out of the nest and pointed at Laz. 'I can

think of something much more likely to be cherished by leprechauns than your coffee and cocoa. That cap on your head! Why don't you offer us *that*?'

An infuriating grin spread over his face. 'The leprechauns don't even remember what makes it special, so how could they cherish it?' He stroked the feather. 'But I'm willing to strike a bargain, Zaria Tourmaline. If Le MoCo doesn't work for the spell, I'll throw in the cap.'

We all looked at him doubtfully. Leona sniffed.

Grabbing my hand, Laz slapped the foil packet into it. 'LeMoCo, Zaria.'

I rubbed the smooth foil with my thumb. Could it possibly work? 'What if you're wrong? We can't waste the other ingredients testing your mixture.'

'It could taint the entire spell,' Meteor said.

Laz smiled too broadly. 'Make up a small batch. I'll volunteer to test it.'

'We can't test it,' I told him. 'The King of the Trolls made me promise that if we make aevia ray, we'll turn it over to King Oberon and Queen Velleron.'

His smile evaporated. 'And you agreed?'

'What?' Leona cried. 'We're taking the aevia ray to the royals? But—'

'The trolls said they'd hold her to her word,' Meteor interrupted. 'And troll magic is much worse than all our fears about it.'

'Delightful,' Laz muttered. 'Better by the minute.'

'They wouldn't give her the Nectara without her promise!' Meteor looked as if he'd like to change Laz into a crock of fermented putch.

'So, if we succeed in making aevia ray, we're taking it to Anshield Island,' I said flatly.

'Well, you can't go through all the trouble of busting into the sapphire stronghold unless you know you have something valuable, can you?' Laz put on a high, whiny voice. 'Your Majesties, I've brought you a magnificent gift of aevia ray — except I don't actually know it's aevia ray. It might be some leftover biscuit crumbs mixed with dust, but I hope you'll like it.' He pretended to grovel in front of an imaginary king and queen.

He'd made his point. 'All right,' I said, fuming. 'We'll test it. But not on you, Laz. Andalonus was born a Red. We'll test the aevia ray on him.'

Laz took on a crafty look. 'Each of us should try a pinch. It's not as if the troll king will ever find out. We could swear each other to secrecy.'

How tempting it was to accept his idea! If our ingredients turned into aevia ray, we'd have plenty. We could give Andalonus vast reserves, and also bring back all the magic my friends and I had used. We could set some aside for my family.

I let myself imagine, but then shook my head. 'The trolls would know. Besides, I pledged my word.'

'In a moment of weakness,' Laz said. 'Under duress.'

'Doesn't matter,' Meteor replied. 'Zaria's word is good.'

'That's why we trust her,' Leona said.

I looked at my friends. How lucky I was. *They* weren't controlled by greed. They cared about me. And about Feyland.

I floated up enough to look down on Laz. 'You're right, the mix should be tested. But one genie will be enough. Andalonus has a better right to it than you.'

'Then I withdraw my offer of Le MoCo.'

Leona laughed. 'Blackmail?'

Laz spoke directly to me. 'Aren't you the good fairy who wants to help your precious Feyland?' he said, as if Feyland had nothing to do with him; as if he didn't live there too. 'You're running out of time, Zaria Tourmaline. Durable spells failing, Galena teeming with malicious gremlins, Lily Morganite flaunting her powers in the open—'

'Stop,' Meteor interrupted. 'You've said enough.'

'I'm doing you a favour,' Laz said solemnly. 'Any test will be risky. Not everyone would volunteer.'

What a trog.

'But if it turns out to be aevia ray,' Leona said, 'you don't deserve to have it.'

I didn't like it either. 'What do you think, Meteor?'

Scowling, he said, 'Make a very small batch. Test it on Laz – and be done with him.'

Laz bowed. 'I pledge to make myself scarce afterwards.'

I floated towards Leona and touched wing tips. 'All right?'

Her eyes were the colour of lead, but she agreed.

'Then,' I said, looking from one to the next, 'let's do this.'

Chapter Thirty-eight

Smugglers have been studied to some extent by several historians, but their code of behaviour follows no discernible pattern. They are greedier than gremlins, persuasive as pixies, and more unpredictable than trolls.

Orville Gold, genie historian of Feyland

I was full of misgivings. If we succeeded in making aevia ray, would a greedy smuggler like Laz be satisfied with 'a pinch'? Wouldn't he try to get control of all he could – one way or another?

I wished he would leave while we mixed the ingredients, but one look at his stubbly jaw told me I'd never persuade him to get out. Curse him and his leprechaun cap!

Leona didn't know him as well as I did. She told him to 'get lost' and then yelled in his face when he wouldn't listen. Laz hovered, lazily grinning, ignoring what she said. Meteor didn't try any more than I did; instead he woke Andalonus and told him what had happened.

Tumble slept through it all.

It was an uneasy gathering when we all came together.

214

Meteor, the one who knew the actual spell for aevia ray from beginning to end, took charge. He began by telling me to fetch a crystal cup and a silver spoon. 'Anything that holds the aevia ray must be made of pure crystal, like our watches.'

I went downstairs and brought out my mother's crystal teacup, a cup that had lived in the back of the cupboard since the day she disappeared. How long ago it seemed now. Even the meeting with my friends in the sonnia field seemed far back in time, as if ten eras had come and gone since then.

I reached for the cup, remembering the way my mother had held it – firmly, yet with gentleness. Her way of drinking tea was one of the few things I could clearly recall about her. I bowed my head for a moment, overcome with missing her.

Rummaging a little more, I found a small crystal flask and used magic to clean it. Then I took up a silver spoon and returned to the others.

Meteor took the items, nodding approval. He directed everyone except the napping gremlin to sit in a circle. The spiral pattern of the tiles on the floor would help us cast the complicated spell, he said.

I lowered myself to a spot on the gleaming tiles. Laz ended up on my left and Meteor on my right. Andalonus was next to Laz on the other side, and Leona between Meteor and Andalonus.

Meteor placed the teacup in the centre of our circle. 'There are five of us,' he said, 'so we'll each look after one of the ingredients.' He brought out the biscuit Tumble had bestowed on me.

I pulled the trolls' present from my pocket and gave it to Leona. 'Nectara.'

Opening the sack, she withdrew a slender jar with a screw-top lid. It appeared to be plain glass made on Earth. The liquid inside was perfectly clear. 'Looks like water,' she said. 'Did the trolls trick you?'

Did they?

I turned to Laz. 'Is it supposed to be clear?'

'Don't know. It appears you'll have to trust the trolls.'

How dare he blather on to me about trust?

'I don't know of any tests for Nectara, so all we can do is try it,' Meteor said. 'The elixir goes in first,' he told Leona. 'Just a drop.'

With steady hands, she unscrewed the lid and allowed a drip to fall into the cup.

'Next the biscuit.' Meteor pinched off a crumb.

'Something cherished by leprechauns.'

Laz sprinkled a dash of Le MoCo.

'Now, the comet dust,' Meteor told me. 'One grain.'

I brought out the vial. Opening it, I caught a whiff of fragrance, the same that I'd sniffed while standing on Earth. Light and darkness collided in my heart, rippling, rushing, turning. I felt as if I were flying at great speeds, seeing stars winking in and out, days and nights merging, fire flashing while ice formed.

I shook a speck into the crystal cup.

Meteor pointed to Andalonus. 'You sing while I stir.'

Andalonus began the song of the pixies, and his singing voice sounded wonderful, as if the pixies had done something to sweeten it.

'*The soft edge of time,*' he sang.
'*is the beginning of the end,*
and the end of the beginning
brings the infinite dawn.'

Using the silver spoon, Meteor mixed the ingredients into a beige paste that barely coated the very bottom of the cup. He stirred till Andalonus sang the final words.

'The last step is to speak the spell.' Meteor pulled a scroll from his genie robe. 'It's quite long, and it will have to be Leona or Zaria because it takes Level One Hundred.'

'Let me. I can spare five hundred thousand radia.' Leona drew her wand.

Meteor held the scroll so Leona and I could both see it. His penmanship was good, but it didn't matter. There were far too many words – arcane words only an ancient scholar would understand. Things like *omtept*, *deromi* and *lrgyslon*.

'I don't recognize anything you've written! Do you

know how to pronounce this gibberish?' Leona asked Meteor after studying the spell.

'Some of it, but not all.'

'Then I can't do it,' Leona said. 'I'd get it wrong.'

She looked at me, and so did everyone else.

'You think I could do a Feynere spell for aevia ray?' I asked. Silence.

Meteor was the first to speak. 'You've opened portals,' he said. 'You've put up a granite wall. You've created protections even gnomes cannot pass.'

Laz raised his eyebrows at that before adding his own comment. 'You've thrown gremlins around like a pack of cards.'

And I created aevum derk.

Laz gave a raspy chuckle. 'My bet's on you, Zaria Tourmaline.'

I waited till I could feel a spark of strength. The others waited too. Not even Laz tried to hurry me. Finally I drew my amethyst wand and infused to Level 100, then tapped the edge of the crystal cup. 'Become aevia ray.'

At first, the paste lay inert in the cup, looking like a smear someone had forgotten to clean. But as we watched, it began to transform. The colour turned from beige to ruby red. Red changed to citrine orange, then rapidly yellow, then green. Blue was there for an instant. Indigo. Violet.

Then the paste became a tiny heap of transparent powder.

'It looks just as the spell described,' Meteor whispered.

I expected Laz to snatch the cup as soon as he believed it held aevia ray, but he surprised me. He bowed from where he sat – bowed as if he meant it, the feather of his cap grazing the floor.

'What shall I do with it?' he asked Meteor respectfully.

'Place it on your tongue.'

'Shouldn't you remove your cap?' Leona sniped. 'Won't it interfere with the enchantment of the aevia ray?'

He grinned at her. 'In a word, no. The cap protects me from spells that oppose me, spells I need protection from. Not aevia ray.' He flipped open his watch. 'In honour of this moment, I will allow you to view my level and colour.' He showed us Level 45, full Yellow.

He picked up the teacup. After shaking the contents onto his blue tongue, he closed his eyes and waited.

I was next to him, so I saw the radia hand on his watch begin to move. It crept from Yellow into the first degree of Green.

I gasped, and the others craned to see. It was happening! We'd done it; we'd created aevia ray, a legendary substance from the ancient past.

Next, the radia hand on Laz's watch jumped from Green to Blue and then Blue to Violet. At the halfway mark of Violet it stopped advancing, quivered, and stood still.

Laz's eyes batted open. When he saw his watch he let out a whoop that woke Tumble.

'Quick,' I urged, pointing to the gremlin who was sitting up and rubbing his eyes. 'Put everything away so he doesn't spill anything.'

We scrambled to stow the ingredients as Tumble climbed down from his window seat and shuffled towards me. He crawled into my lap.

'A sneaking smuggler has more radia than me,' Leona blazed; 'more than a real Violet fairy.'

Laz winked wickedly. 'Do you still believe you should take the entire batch to Anshield? Remember, every one of you could be full Violet and have plenty left over for their majesties.' He saluted Leona. 'Small consolation, I know, my lovely – but if you'll notice, it didn't raise my level, only my *reserves* of magic. When it comes to levels, you're still the most powerful fairy in the land.' He showed his watch around again, and sure enough, the level had remained at 45.

I was very relieved that Laz would never be able to make himself invisible – which was a Level 50 spell. If he could, I'd have to be looking over my wings every minute. Bad enough that his cap let him traipse through my defences whenever it suited him. Oh yes, I was glad the aevia ray hadn't raised Laz's Level. But at the same time, I felt sad knowing that even if Andalonus took aevia ray, he'd never make a single journey to Earth.

Chapter Thirty-nine

THE UNKNOWN SURROUNDS US, EVEN AFTER PARTS OF IT
BECOME KNOWN.

Orville Gold, genie historian of Feyland

Tumble began playing with the cover on my watch,
snapping it open and closed, reminding me to check my
radia reserves.

'Five hundred thousand radia to make aevia ray,' I
announced. 'Just what Meteor said it would be.'

Laz lurched to his feet. 'As promised, I must be going.'

'That's it?' Leona hooted. 'Without a word of thanks?'

'I was under the impression you wanted me to leave.'

'But Zaria just spent five hundred thousand radia – on
you. You owe her!'

He flicked the rim of his cap. 'Sometimes I gamble and
win.' He looked down at me. 'Best of luck, Zaria
Tourmaline, keeping your word to the trolls. And watch out
for that Morganite creature.'

'Wait, Laz.' Something about what he said bothered me.
'Why do you always call her that? What does it mean?' His
face was much too innocent. 'You know something.' I was
suddenly sure of it.

He half closed his eyes and didn't answer.

'Laz? Who *is* she?'

'A shame you didn't ask earlier.' He clicked his tongue. 'Our bargain expired yesterday evening.'

'Bargain?' I asked foolishly.

'I agreed to answer any question for fifty radia – for three days.'

I smiled. 'You're five million radia richer! That should be worth a lot more answers.'

I waited for his return smile, but it didn't come. 'No, no, my fine fairy. You keep to your code; I keep to mine. And the code of a gambler says: just because you win big doesn't mean you give anything away.'

I couldn't believe it. I really could not. I glared at the smuggler, while Tumble squeaked softly in my lap. My friends' faces showed speechless outrage.

'So much for your grand offer of service,' I said. Setting Tumble beside me, I rose to face Laz. 'I'll pay you. Who is Lily Morganite?'

He leaned towards me, his skinny nose almost poking my forehead. 'That's a million-radia question, and I won't answer it for less.'

Leona was up, her wand out and infused.

'Leona!' I waved frantically at Laz's cap.

She hovered, raging, trying to pull the magic back out of her wand.

Meteor burst towards Laz, and so did Andalonus. They

crashed, not into the smuggler but into each other, for Laz was no longer there.

'Rotten trog!' Leona fumed.

When the genies disentangled themselves, Andalonus bent and picked up the shiny foil packet of Le MoCo. 'At least he left this behind.'

Meteor began pummelling the air where the smuggler had been. 'You're right, Zaria. That genie knows something about Lily Morganite. Something important.'

I nodded, furious that he'd swindled me again. 'Do *you* know anything?' I asked Meteor. 'Anything you haven't told us?'

He clutched his striped hair. 'Only what everyone knows – that she became a member of the High Council decades ago, and then Forcier of Feyland ten years back. No children. No record of who her parents are or when she was born.'

I sank glumly into my mother's nest. Tumble jumped up beside me to roll on the silky pillows. 'Maybe we *should* use the aevia ray ourselves. Then, not only could we renew the durable spells and give radia to every fairy and genie, but we could force Laz to tell us what he knows.'

Meteor shook his head back and forth so hard it looked like it might fly off his neck. 'What would the trolls do to you if you broke your word?'

What *would* they do? They'd proven they had no trouble overriding my magic. Did I have to be in their presence before they could invade my mind? What if they could control me no matter where I went? How would I live if I couldn't do the simplest thing unless a troll first agreed?

Leona touched a wing tip to mine. 'We can't lose you to the trolls.'

Meteor nodded. 'They might accept one small test, but it would be dangerous to take any for ourselves.'

'We have to take the aevia ray to Anshield, Zaria,' said Andalonus. 'For your sake.'

'For your sake,' Tumble chirped.

I sighed. 'Let's make the full batch, then.'

Tumble returned to the window seat and began unpacking sacks of biscuits. Each taste brought on a loud, happy whistle from the little gremlin. But as we prepared to make more aevia ray, he went to sleep again.

The only difficult thing about creating the larger batch was being patient as Meteor insisted we measure drops and crumbs, grains and specks. When we finished, the comet dust was the only ingredient completely used up – there were quite a few biscuit crumbs, most of the packet of Le MoCo, and nearly a whole bottle of Nectara to spare.

The little crystal flask was almost full. Meteor had predicted that although we'd be creating at least ten thousand times more aevia ray than we did for the test batch, performing the spell would use the same amount of radia the second time. He was right.

I half expected Laz to appear in the doorway before I could seal the flask, but he didn't. 'No one and nothing but me can break or open this flask,' I said. 'No one and nothing can take this aevia ray without my agreement.'

For a while we just sat on the bright tiles, four friends united by exhaustion and elation. We had created something impossibly rare. We should be celebrating, singing from the rooftops, dancing in the air. Yet none of us showed any glee — we were all more ready to cry than to sing; more ready to sleep than to dance.

'It's so unfair,' Leona grumbled. 'Zaria, you risked your life and your magic for aevia ray. And the only one who benefits is that greedy smuggler!'

'You risked a lot too,' I said, looking from one to the next.

Meteor sighed. 'Laz is gone, and we should go too.' He rose from the floor.

I looked over at Tumble, sprawled peacefully among his biscuit crumbs, snoring noisily. I longed to curl up beside him and find my own dreams. 'So how do we get to Anshield?' I asked wearily.

'I suppose I could transport to the sapphire gate.' Meteor sounded equally weary. 'My father told me exactly where it is.'

'He *told* you?' Andalonus asked

Meteor rubbed his forehead. 'Odd for him to break the secrecy of the council, but after what happened with Lily, he made me repeat the directions back to him so I wouldn't forget.'

An uneasy feeling crawled over my wings. Did Councillor Zircon expect to die? Why else would he reveal such a secret to his son?

But Leona was focused on Anshield. She raised her wand, its filigree flashing. 'I can easily transport all of us. Tell me how to get there.'

We listened closely as Meteor described where we were headed. 'Anshield Island is in the middle of Glendonite Lake. Between the shores of the lake and the sapphire gate there's a wide stretch of white sand. The gate's three wingspans wide and four high – and it's the only way through the wall around the stronghold.'

'The only way?' Leona asked.

'The wall's enchanted so no one can fly over it or transport past it.'

'Maybe I could,' I said. 'Transport inside the gate with a Feynere spell.'

'No,' Meteor answered hastily. 'That would be as dangerous as transporting from world to world. You wouldn't know where – or when – you'd land. The enchantments on that island change time itself, in ways I do not understand.'

'We'll go to the gate then,' Leona declared.

I looked at Tumble again. What would happen to him if he wandered outside while we were gone? 'What should we do with the gremlin?'

'We can't leave him behind,' Leona said briskly, as if it was completely normal for her to care about a gremlin. 'He's hardly more than a baby.'

'We could take him with us,' Andalonus suggested. 'He could ride in that human-made backpack.'

While Andalonus roused Tumble and helped him climb into the pack, I used Feynere magic to seal the leftover ingredients for aevia ray into a cupboard – the Nectara, the remains of the special biscuit, and Le MoCo.

The crystal flask I slid into the deepest pocket of my gown, then handed Tumble another biscuit.

'Ready?' Leona infused her wand to Level 20.

Andalonus strapped on the pack that held the gremlin. Tumble whistled excitedly as the four of us joined hands.

'*Transera nos*,' Leona said.

Chapter Forty

Humans are unaware that they are dependent upon fey folk to keep from becoming too downcast and hardened.

The human world is overburdened with a certain type of reality that has strict laws of physics, heavy and solid. The fey world is more effervescent and airy; on Tirfeyne the laws of physics are more yielding and responsive.

Encounters with magic (so long as that magic is not of the wicked, malicious variety) are beneficial to humans, allowing them relief from the more ponderous aspects of existence.

Orville Gold, genie historian of Feyland

I bumped into someone, hard.

'Oof!' I huffed, and found myself nose-to-nose with none other than Magistria Lodestone, head of the High Council of Feyland.

A ruby of Oberon, the symbol of power she always wore, glinted at her throat. Beside her was Meteor's father,

Councillor Zircon. His own ruby of Oberon was set in a heavy bracelet on his wrist.

'Zaria?' The magistria's obsidian eyes darted over my companions. 'Leona Bloodstone? Meteor, and—? Oberon's Crown, Andalonus Copper, what *is* that on your back?' The hefty fairy recoiled at the sight of Tumble, who started squeaking.

I patted his head to calm him but he grabbed my hand and scrambled out of the pack. He slid to the ground and scurried off to huddle in the shadow of a wall – a wall of luminous blue ten wingspans high.

We had arrived at the royal stronghold.

Looking behind us, I saw a lakeshore and a swathe of sand, each grain shimmering so sharply that I had to shade my eyes. A dazzling mist crouched over the waters.

Anshield's shores should have been a beautiful sight, something to charm my memory for years. It wasn't. Already, I hoped to forget I had ever seen this island. Something was wrong, something besides the painfully bright sand and mist. Was it because of the enchantments? Spells that altered time itself would create a peculiar feeling, wouldn't they?

I turned back to the magistria and the councillor. If I had followed proper manners, I would have bowed to them. I didn't, and neither did my friends. Perhaps that explained why Councillor Zircon gave us no greeting and frowned at his son, saying only, 'What are you doing here?'

'We need to get in,' Meteor said. 'Why are *you* here?'

Zircon glanced at the magistria. 'We have important messages for their majesties, of course,' he answered, voice grim. 'But what could you possibly—'

'Then why are you *outside* the gate?' Meteor interrupted.

'The gate will not open,' the magistria explained. 'Our passwords have failed.'

Zircon shifted uneasily, one foot hugging the other. The movement drew my attention to his feet. And his boots.

Green boots, rather new. And suddenly I was back in the grove on Earth, huddled beneath the blue spruce, listening to Lily as she stole the aevum derk, watching the boots of the councillor who had spoken only in whispers.

'You,' I said, glaring at his boots.

When I lifted my eyes, everyone else was frowning. At me.

I pointed at Zircon. 'He's the one who was there. With Lily. *With* her. When she took the indigo bottle.'

'Nonsense,' Zircon answered, his feet burrowing into the sand.

I heard a sharp intake of breath from Meteor. 'You worked with *her*?' he asked his father.

'Of course not.' Zircon scowled.

The magistria grabbed her ruby pendant; against her stark white skin it appeared even redder than usual. 'I myself asked Councillor Zircon to observe Lily Morganite's movements,' she said haughtily. 'How did *you* know about Lily's weapon, Zaria?'

'Her weapon!' I gasped. 'Has she opened it?'

No answer.

Meteor was watching his father the way he had watched Laz, distrust drawn over his face like a mask.

'Has she opened the bottle?' I was almost screaming.

'Not yet,' Magistria Lodestone answered. 'She will spare Feyland a while longer, but how—'

'Spare?' I shouted. 'She—'

Meteor moved closer to me. I felt him take my hand and squeeze.

'Zaria? What do you know of the indigo bottle?' The magistria's black wings expanded, making a sharp outline against the blue of the gate.

'I know Lily Morganite has it, and—' I stopped again, clinging to Meteor's hand.

Pebbly black eyes peered at me. A few days ago, the magistria would have threatened me with iron shackles if I had refused to answer her. But all she said now was, 'Keeping secrets can be dangerous, child.'

Child. It seemed that whenever powerful fairies or genies wanted something from me, they forgot my name and used the word *child*.

Zircon spoke up. 'You have not told us why you wanted to see the king and queen.'

'You haven't told us why your passwords won't open the

gate,' Meteor answered, dropping my hand to draw his wand.

The magistria heaved a gusty sigh. 'It is a mystery, young Zircon. And without the king and queen, the council does not have the strength to save Feyland.'

Meteor's father glided closer to her and whispered something.

Nodding pompously, the magistria spoke directly to Leona. 'Dire times call for dire measures. Leona Bloodstone, perhaps your high-level magic would be of help here.'

Leona already had her wand out, but she kicked at the sand and took a moment to answer. 'You're asking me to break into the sapphire stronghold?'

Zircon rested his palm against the polished stone of the gate. 'We have tried everything.'

Before Leona could say more, Meteor raised a hand. 'Something's wrong.' He aimed his wand at the magistria and his father. 'You've both studied the lore of Anshield Island.'

Magistria Lodestone held onto her ruby. 'Of course.'

'Then you know that no amount of fey magic can open the sapphire gate from the outside. No amount. Even if Leona used Level Two Hundred, her magic would still be fey.'

'What?' I blurted, and heard my question echoed by Andalonus and Leona. 'Why didn't you tell us this before? How will we get in?'

Meteor glanced at me and clamped his lips. Of course, that meant everyone else decided to stare at me.

'Zaria?' Magistria Lodestone asked greedily. 'Can *you* open the gate?'

Meteor grabbed my hand again and pulled me out of earshot of the others. 'Troll magic,' he said, his mouth very close to my ear. 'Your troll wish could easily open the gate.'

'I don't want to use it here! And I don't trust the magistria or—'

'I don't trust them either, Zaria. But it's true they need to tell the king and queen about what's happening in Feyland. And we need to get in too.'

'Then I'll use a Feynere spell to open the gate.'

His eyes reflected the sand's harsh sparkle. 'A Feynere is still fey.'

Blast Meteor! Why did he read so many scrolls? And why had the trolls told me about their 'one wish' while he was listening? Who would know better than Meteor that troll magic was nothing like fey magic?

Blast the trolls too! Had they foreseen this? When they said the wish must be from my heart, had they known I would be caught this way, with the future of Feyland weighing on my wings? They had extorted a promise from me to deliver the aevia ray to Feyland's rulers. Now, to keep that promise I would need their 'one wish'.

A wish of my heart. What was more important, finding my family or saving Feyland? I felt as if two trolls stood beside me, pulling my wings in different directions.

One side held memories of my family as it used to be. And although I had driven most of those memories away when I thought they were dead, a few remained. I thought of my mother brewing tea and serving it with gentle haste before she flew to the Golden Station; of my father fixing our family clock with a flick of his wand; of my brother Jett telling me that although prisms would split light into beauty, crystal watches split Feyland into ugliness.

It didn't seem possible that I could want anything more than I wanted them home again.

But on the other side, I remembered Feyland as it used to be. I thought of growing up in Galena with my friends, playing leaping genie on the soft sands, viewing the glittering roofs from above as we learned to fly. We had never needed to spare a thought for our safety there. And now, with the gateway spells broken, that safety had fled. I brought to mind the shining scopes that fey folk had used for millennia to watch over their human godchildren on Earth. If the scopes were never repaired and the portals stayed closed, the connection between our world and the human world would end.

If I didn't open the gate, didn't give the rightful rulers the aevia ray, how much longer would it be before Feyland disappeared like coloured smoke? *The outcome will determine whether fey magic will endure or sink into nothingness* – or so the King of the Trolls had said.

I felt as if someone had thrown burning handfuls of sand in my eyes. 'You're right,' I whispered to Meteor.

Very gently, he wiped my tears with his thumbs. 'Zaria, I . . .'

From the moment the King of the Trolls had ordered me to take the aevia ray to Anshield Island, Meteor must have guessed my 'one wish' would go to Feyland. I knew he wanted me to say I didn't begrudge the way he had kept the truth about the gate from me. But I couldn't.

We flew back to the others in silence.

'Well?' asked the magistria.

'I carry troll magic,' I told her slowly. 'I can open the gate.'

'Troll magic!' she exclaimed. 'My dear child.'

'I am not your *child*.'

'Well, my dear, it's just—'

'And I am not your dear! So if you want me to do this, get back from the gate. I don't want you breathing down my wings.'

The magistria looked as if she'd like to grind me under her heel, but I didn't care. I clearly remembered the troll telling me that the one wish must be *a wish of your heart* – and as long as the magistria was anywhere near, my heart would not be able to feel anything but anger and disgust.

Councillor Zircon whispered to her again, his hand on her arm as he steered her away, down the sand towards the lakeshore. Taking bitter satisfaction in her fury, I waved them further on until they hovered at the water's edge.

Then my friends gathered close and waited quietly until I was ready.

I spoke. 'I wish this sapphire gate to open.'

I should have been more careful. I should have laid out who could enter the gate and who could not. I should have remembered all the warnings about troll magic.

If I had, I would have said something different. I wouldn't have made one of the biggest mistakes of my life.

Chapter Forty-one

Humans who possess enough magic sometimes find their way into Feyland through unguarded portals. When they do, they carry tales to Earth, tales of unimaginable riches. They speak of the Cities of Gold, the Fountain of Youth, the Shangri-la. Those who get a glimpse of Feyland will spend the rest of their lives trying to find it again unless placed under a forgetting spell.

Orville Gold, genie historian of Feyland

The gate swung open.

Just beyond was a field of flowers holding every variety of blossom I had ever seen as well as some that were new to me. A thousand shades of colour swayed under the great sky. A long way off, the distant spires of a sapphire palace caught the light, reflecting it back as if offering a splendid promise.

But there were no fairies or genies on guard at the gate, no one tending the flowers. The king and queen must be very confident in their defences. What if I had been someone else, someone who wanted them overthrown?

As if my fears had taken form, I heard a laugh just behind

me, a familiar laugh that stung my ears like icy water. A cloying scent fogged over me. Lilies.

Slowly I revolved and let my feet touch the ground. At that moment, I didn't trust my wings to hold me aloft. My friends turned with me, wands out. Even Andalonus drew his simple Level 4 wand.

Magistria Lodestone hovered in front of us, pleased and smiling. I looked past her but saw no one else.

'Magistria?' I said. 'Did you hear . . . ?'

'Thank you, Zaria,' she said.

As the scent of lilies intensified, the magistria's face blurred like a painting smeared with oil. Her eyes were different. No longer chips of obsidian, they changed to gloating pearls. Black wings became white. Chalky skin pinkened.

Lily Morganite. A satiny gown draped her in a colour she favoured: shell pink. Opalescent jewels studded her saffron hair.

I fell, kneeling in the sand at her feet before Meteor pulled me up.

Lily glided past us through the gate, then turned and flew out again, smiling. 'How good of you to give me what I wanted most, Zaria,' she said.

I leaned against Meteor. How easily I had done as Lily wished! How could I have missed her desire to invade this place? She and Zircon had played me for a fool. Perfectly.

Zircon! Where was he? I looked for him but saw only

the beach and the empty water. What was his part in all this? He had told his son how to find the stronghold, and well he knew that Meteor and I were friends. But he couldn't have known that I held a wish from the trolls.

Confusion and anger pushed against each other in my heart, and my Feynere magic flickered. Sliding my hand in my pocket, I touched my wand. Usually it brought a feeling of strength, but now it only kept me from collapsing again.

'Better yet, you've brought me a gift,' Lily said. 'Aevia ray.'

'No.' My wings felt like dead leaves, their margins dragging the ground.

'I could not have done it without you.' Lily raised her wand delicately. 'At first, I followed you in case you needed help when you robbed the humans.'

You couldn't. I was invisible.

'You are not the only one, Zaria, who can use humans for information,' she continued. 'All I needed was to locate the comet dust and wait – for you.'

I had acted as fast as I could to stay ahead of her. But Lily, a beautiful fairy with decades of experience *using humans*, had been ahead of me all along. Watching.

I remembered the coffee bean that had spooked Laz in his portal room. Had Lily been there after all?

Had there ever been a time when she might have seen me with Sam? What if she knew who he was, where he lived?

'I never doubted you, Zaria. But waiting at this gate took longer than I would have liked,' Lily said sweetly. 'So, I am ready for my gift. Now.'

How had she known I would come to Anshield carrying aevia ray? I considered Laz but dismissed him; he hated 'the Morganite' for double-crossing him. Was Lily working with the trolls, then? I would never have come here, never have opened the gate for her, if it hadn't been for my promise to the King of the Trolls and his gift of the one wish. Had they plotted together to bring me to this moment?

However it had come about, there was nothing to be gained from staying here another instant. It was time for me and my friends to transport away.

Gripping my wand in one hand and Meteor's arm in the other, I nodded to Leona, who had no trouble understanding what I meant. She nodded back and touched Andalonus's shoulder.

'Before you go,' Lily said. 'I have something to show you.'

We paused as she lifted her wand and infused the smoky quartz rod. Turning her back, she waved at the shore. '*Chantmentum pellex,*' she cried.

The reversal spell.

A row of fairies and genies appeared, hovering above the sand. I vaguely recognized some of them from the attack on my home.

Behind them, more appeared, and some of these I had seen almost every day of my life: fey folk from Galena who had endured gremlins ransacking their homes, and then begged me for refuge.

Refuge I had refused.

Wave after wave, row upon row of fairies and genies showed themselves as Lily's spells of invisibility dropped away. In moments, she revealed an army streaming towards us. I couldn't count them all.

Nor could I count how much radia she must have used to hide so many.

'Now!' she called, dipping her wand.

Her followers didn't shout as they rushed, didn't scream or roar. But the sound of their wings beating and robes swishing took over the sky. My friends and I barely had time to dodge as Lily's army drove past us through the gate to the sapphire stronghold. They never looked aside.

When the last one had crossed the gateway and joined the swarm heading towards the palace, Lily turned to me. 'Yes,' she said. 'They will open the way for me.'

Feynere magic simmered beneath my skin. I should dash through the gate, chase down that army, stop them, let my powers trample them into the field of flowers. They would never take orders from Lily Morganite again.

Meteor's fingers dug into my side. 'Don't listen,' he said, low and soothing.

I fastened myself desperately to his voice. *No, no*, I told my magic. *Lily is goading me. Remember what happened among the trolls.*

'I will command their return,' Lily was saying. 'But only for the aevia ray.'

'Never.' I tried hard to give strength to the small word but it sounded weak and afraid.

'Then allow me to provide another inducement.' Lily swished her wand again. '*Revelum nos.*' The reveal spell.

Five wingspans away, two burly genies appeared. I recognized one as the fellow with granite-grey skin who had sneered at me back in Galena. The other had yellow skin dotted with black. Propped between them was another genie, shorter and smaller, with reddish-gold hair.

No, not a genie. A human.

Sam.

Chapter Forty-two

IN THE ONGOING CONNECTION BETWEEN THE WORLDS
OF TIRFEYNE AND EARTH, HUMANS AND FEY FOLK ARE
ESPECIALLY CLOSE. IT IS A TERRIBLE BREACH OF THAT
CONNECTION FOR A MEMBER OF THE FEY TO KILL A
HUMAN BEING. EQUALLY HEINOUS IS FOR A HUMAN TO
MURDER A FAIRY OR GENIE.

Orville Gold, genie historian of Feyland

Sam! His mouth moved without making a sound. Gag
spell? Either that, or he was too overcome to speak.
The grey genie had something pressed against his temple,
something I had seen before: the laser gun I had buried on
Earth.

'This human means something to you.' Lily gave me an
acrid smile.

I fluttered towards Sam, my wings beating raggedly.

'*Chantmentum pellex*,' I said softly to release him from any
gag spell, and sent magic into the wand still in my pocket.

He squinted hard at me. 'Those eyes,' he said, his voice
cracking. 'You look like a lot like that girl I met named
Zaria – only you have wings and . . .'

I wanted to touch him, comfort him, but I simply hovered, and didn't answer.

'I'm dreaming, aren't I?' he asked. 'But I don't remember falling asleep.' He tried to lift his hand, but the genies on either side of him pinned his arms to his sides. 'What the . . . ?' he said, and then stared round wildly, while I watched in helpless fear.

Lily floated close to us, her heavy scent strangling. 'Aevia ray, Zaria, or say a last goodbye to this pitiful human.'

Sam nodded to himself. 'Definitely dreaming.'

Pouring power into my hidden wand, I spoke aloud a spell using ordinary words: 'The gun is useless.'

'Wrong,' Lily answered, pointing to the grey genie. 'Calcite tested it.'

How had he tested it? Had he hurt someone? If only I had destroyed the gun sooner.

'I know your affection for this human.' She touched Sam's forehead with a graceful finger, and he flinched and shut his eyes.

How had she found him? There were so few times when I could have been seen in the scopes with Sam, each lasting only seconds.

What could I do for him now? Even if I struck a bargain for his freedom, Lily would remember where he lived and who he was. *Unless I can get past her protection spells.* Again, I felt the wild Feynere magic flaring.

Leona drifted forward with Andalonus, watchful and

waiting. *Please, Leona. Please. Take this human boy away from here. Take him to safety.*

My fairy friend gave me a sad smile – and then vanished with Andalonus.

Lily sniffed triumphantly. 'One by one, Zaria, your friends desert you.'

But the grey genie yelled as he smacked into his fellow captor.

Sam too was gone.

Leona had understood me! She had understood, and transported Sam and Andalonus beyond the reach of Lily Morganite.

Lily's glossy white wings rippled, while the rest of her stiffened. 'Leona Bloodstone, wasting radia on a human?' For a moment she seemed unable to take it in. Had we, at last, done something she hadn't foreseen?

Then she wrenched the gun from Calcite's hand, aimed at Meteor and pulled the trigger. I heard a popping click. No deadly red beam, no harm to Meteor.

Lily flung the weapon on the ground. I expected her to rage at Calcite and toss an enchantment over him to show her fury. She didn't. Instead, she drifted even closer to me. 'Human weapons are unreliable,' she said. 'But fey enchantments are something to be counted on.'

We had to get away and deliver the aevia ray to the king and queen. I would use a Feynere spell to find them, and transport myself and Meteor to wherever they were.

'Yes,' Lily was saying. 'Unlike human weapons, fey enchantments never change. The glacier spell, for example.'

I froze.

'It cannot be undone except by the the one who casts it,' Lily said, and then waved her wand. '*Revelum nos.*'

In the shadow of the great sapphire wall behind her, two pallets appeared, long and narrow slabs of granite resting in the sand. On one lay a genie, on the other a fairy.

My wings snapped open and I flew so fast I would have slammed into the granite if Meteor hadn't grabbed me back at the last moment.

'Don't!' he yelled, yanking on my wings. 'Don't let the glacier cloth touch you.'

I reeled, but Meteor didn't let go – he forced me to the ground a wingspan from the pallets. I trembled in his grasp, staring at my father and mother.

Their faces and the tips of my mother's golden-yellow wings were the only parts of their bodies not covered. Everything else was wrapped in something that looked as if it had been woven from threads of ice.

They lay much too still. I wanted to throw myself onto them, but two things stopped me. Their eyes. And Meteor.

My parents' eyes revealed the depths of their enchantment. Open, but glazed and fixed as if caught in the flow of a glacier.

Meteor's feet pinned my gown; his hands clamped my

wrists. 'The spell will spread if it touches any part of you,' he said.

I gazed at my mother's lavender skin, silky white hair, tipped-up nose. My father's deep green colouring contrasted with his purple hair. His hair was mussed, and looking at him, I remembered it was always like that, never smooth.

How had I lived without them? I wanted to reach back in time, change the moment of their capture, persuade them not to leave. If only there were a spell to take me to the day before they disappeared! I would warn my brother too. Whatever his quest had been, I would ask him to delay.

But now I was looking at only two pallets. Where was the third?

'Where's Jett?' I cried.

Lily glided up to hover near my mother's head, but she didn't answer me.

The Feynere magic lurking in my bones called out to me. I could undo this horrifying spell and then turn it on Lily Morganite. I could.

My wrists throbbed. 'Meteor, let go.'

But he didn't listen. 'Don't, Zaria,' he whispered urgently in my ear.

He must know then what I wanted; must know that soon I would have no choice: my Feynere powers would rise and burn through all the magic I had left.

His hand found mine, squeezing with painful force until I gasped; he held me close, rocking me.

'Your mother,' I heard Lily saying. 'For the aevia ray.'

'My family,' I cried. 'There are three of them.'

'You may have one.' She lifted her wand. Staring, I saw each opal that crusted her slippers, every small fold in her gown, all the strands in her saffron hair.

'No! You would do anything for aevia ray,' I screamed.

'Not so.' She gestured at the open gateway. 'I have all that I need.' A lock of her hair was loose; she thrust it into place. 'But you, Zaria – *you* – would do anything to have your mother back.'

How could she know? I missed my father, missed my brother, but . . . Dread crackled along the margins of my wings. How did Lily Morganite always seem to guess exactly how I felt and what I would do?

'I want them all,' I said. 'All three.'

Infusion crept up the centre of her wand. 'Must I teach you the value of one?' She pointed her wand and spoke a spell I didn't know. '*Kenor mortel.*'

A smoky dagger formed in the air above my father's chest.

'Stop!' I cried. 'Stop.'

'Your mother for the aevia ray?' The dagger's edge sharpened.

'Yes! Yes, I'll give it to you, but don't kill him.'

Meteor went still, so still he might have been frozen along with my parents. His hand opened, freeing my fingers. But Lily only smiled gloatingly, as if she had known all along how easily I would give in.

Chapter Forty-three

LOVE IS THE GREATEST POWER EVER DISCOVERED, SURPASSING EVEN MAGIC. THIS HOLDS TRUE NOT ONLY FOR THOSE WHO INHABIT TIRFEYNE, BUT ALSO FOR THE PEOPLE OF EARTH.

WHEN GIVEN A CHOICE BETWEEN ACTING FOR THE WELFARE OF MANY NAMELESS STRANGERS OR SECURING THE SAFETY OF A SINGLE LOVED ONE, ALMOST EVERYONE — WHETHER HUMAN OR FEY — WILL CHOOSE THE LATTER. THIS IS WELL KNOWN TO ANYONE WHO HAS STUDIED HISTORY.

Orville Gold, genie historian of Feyland

My wings prickled fiercely as I fully understood what I had agreed to do. In desperation, I had offered something that wasn't mine to give. The aevia ray didn't belong to me, any more than Lily's stolen radia belonged to her.

I looked at the grains of sand stretching to the water, the field of waving flowers beyond the gate, the far-away spires of the palace. What was happening within its walls? What orders had Lily given her army? I could see nothing of them, hear nothing of what they might be doing. Had they breached the royal defences?

Were there any defences aside from enchantments? And how much did Lily know about the spells encircling Anshield Island?

If only the king and queen would come out of their palace, soar past the flowers, fly through the gate.

Help me!

But the sand stayed flat, the gate silent, the flowers quiet. There was nothing and no one to save me.

I would have to save myself. I, Zaria Tourmaline, would have to save my family. But not like this. Not trading the aevia ray to Lily. I would rather hand over the crystal flask to a mercenary smuggler like Laz than give it to Lily Morganite. It was simply too precious, a treasure greater than any other in Feyland. Of all fairies, Lily must never get hold of it.

But without aevia ray, how could I persuade her to release the glacier spells?

I would have to double-cross *Lily*.

Dropping my eyes, I clutched my hidden wand and infused it, whispering a spell: 'In the left pocket of my gown, duplicate the appearance of the crystal flask of aevia ray and seal it.'

'What?' Meteor whispered back.

'Nothing,' I murmured as Lily looked at me suspiciously. My fingers brushed the contours of a second flask – this one on my left side. The true aevia ray nestled on my right. Feeling the false flask, I was suddenly panting, and though I tried to breathe more evenly, I couldn't.

'What is it?' Lily asked.

I planned to give her the false flask for my mother and then offer to open it in trade for my father.

'Please,' I said. 'My mother.'

'Show me the aevia ray,' Lily said.

I brought out the newly created flask, so clear and beautifully cut, it could have been a diamond.

'Give it to me.' Her hand was out.

'No.' I put it back. 'First, my mother.'

Nothing showed on her face as she turned to my parents. Blowing on her wand, she pointed it. '*Chantmentum glaci res nos.*'

The ghastly fabric wrapping my mother began to unwind, slithering into the sand, forming a pale twist at the foot of her pallet. I streaked to her side, flopping to my knees in time to see the film over her eyes melt away.

'Zaria?' Her first word in five years: my name, spoken faintly.

'Yes. It's me.' I took her hand. How dry it was, like kindling.

'My Zaria?' Fear in her eyes. 'What has happened to you?'

Before I could answer, Lily was there beside us, her scent suffocating.

My mother began to whimper, trying to sit up. As I helped her, she clung to me, pulling me forward. 'Zaria,' she whispered, 'that fairy . . . she . . .'

'I know,' I said. 'I know who she is, Mother. I know what she's done.'

Her wings drooped, limp and lustreless. 'Glacier cloth,' she said. 'How long?'

'Five years.'

My mother took in the high blue wall, the glinting sand. In a moment she would turn her head enough to see my father. 'What is this place? This is not where we were . . .' Her voice trembled. 'Where is Jett? Your father? Are they—'

'Enough.' Lily's voice sliced the air. 'Our bargain, Zaria.'

Clutching me, my mother shook her head. She began to shiver as I pulled away from her and rose. Her wings stirred faintly. Clearly, she didn't have the strength to rise, but she called to me. 'Fly from her, Zaria!'

I took the false flask from my pocket again. Lily was watching me, watching closely as she swooped in to snatch it. Holding it up to the light, she looked at the transparent granules glowing inside. They seemed identical to the real aevia ray. She tugged on the stopper; when it wouldn't open, she nodded her satisfaction.

Just then, a flashing blur leaped at her. Something bumped my hand. The next instant, I was holding the flask again.

I heard an exuberant whistle. Tumble! The little gremlin thought he was helping me.

'Run!' I cried, but he was already gone. I glimpsed him

racing through the gate and then he was lost among the flowers.

'After him!' Lily ordered the spotted genie.

As her minion zoomed through the gate after Tumble, I touched my wand. 'He will not find the gremlin,' I murmured, and released more magic.

In that moment of distraction, the other genie, Calcite, pounced on me from the side, grabbing the flask that Tumble had given me. Maybe he expected me to be holding it more tightly, or maybe he simply misjudged his leap. Either way, Calcite used too much force. Instead of giving the flask to Lily Morganite, he crashed past her into the sapphire wall.

When the crystal hit, it shattered, exploding into a shower of sparkling shards, spraying the wall with a fine powder. Calcite fell backwards onto the sand.

When I had sealed the flask, I had not made it unbreakable.

While Meteor and I wobbled forward, Lily lurched into the wall. She licked the powder, then turned back to us and flipped open her crystal watch. Her beautiful face hardened as she infused her wand.

She whirled and pointed at my father. '*Chantmentum glaci res nos.*'

In joyful shock, I watched as the glacier cloth fell from him, watched as his vision cleared. He saw me. His eyes, violet like mine, widened. His lips formed my name.

253

I was so dazed with happiness, I didn't move. Didn't act. Didn't speak.

'*Kenor mortel deysu.*' Lily's voice rang like steel, and I turned to her in confusion. Her wand was extended, its tip aimed at my father.

The smoky dagger appeared above him. This time, it didn't hang in the air. It dived into his chest.

He was just beginning to sit up, still looking at me. The dagger thrust him down and pinned him. His arms thrashed once and then he lay flat. The light in his eyes went out.

No breath. No movement. No life.

A long wail, two voices hitting the same note of rending grief.

Two voices. My mother. Me.

'Why?' Meteor's question was a rumbling roaring yell. It startled me because he had never yelled that way, never, not in all the years I had known him.

He was still beside me, but upright, while I had folded forward onto the sand. When I lifted my head, I saw Lily Morganite above us, her face pulsing with rage.

'If you had kept up with your studies, young Zircon, you would know he could not die outside of time.' Her voice swelled like an angry wind, louder than my mother's wails. '*That* is why.'

'You—' Meteor's voice choked off.

'How dare you try a Feynere fraud again?' Lily shouted

down at me. 'Did you think I would not know? Your foolish trick with the human weapon only removed my last doubts about what you are!'

My mouth tasted of grit. She knew. *Feynere*.

'The true aevia ray, Zaria. Now!' Lily's wand was fully infused. '*Kenor mortel.*' A second dagger appeared just above my mother.

'Wait!' I floundered in the sand, my gown tangled. I had to find the pocket, the right one. The aevia ray.

There. There it was, the crystal flask. Fumbling, shaking, I lifted it up, and Lily took it.

This time, there was no Tumble to rescue it; there was only Lily and her triumph. She pulled on the stopper, but of course she couldn't open it. She bashed it against the sapphire wall, but it didn't break. It chimed like a perfect bell.

No one and nothing but me can break or open this flask.

'Now, Zaria,' she said. 'For your brother, you will open this flask and you will open the bottle of aevum derk.'

Chapter Forty-four

TO GAIN LOVE IS TO GAIN MORE THAN LOVE. AND LOVE,
ONCE BROUGHT TO LIFE, DOES NOT DIE BUT TRANSCENDS
ALL WORLDS, ALL PLACES AND ALL TIMES. SOME DISPUTE
THIS, BUT SUCH DISPUTE DOES NOT ALTER ITS TRUTH.

Orville Gold, genie historian of Feyland

Flashing silver, a colour I loved. Dark hair against granite.
A whispered spell. '*Transera nos.*'

Leona.

And in the same instant, Meteor's hand on my shoulder.
'*Transera nos.*'

They took my mother and me away from Anshield.

We landed on the spiral pattern of tiles in my mother's
room, and there we lay, weeping, gasping, clutching the
floor as if it might turn to sand.

Someone was stroking my hair. It should be my mother.
She was here, really here, the one I'd longed for, whose
guidance would help me through my troubles.

But the soothing hand on my head wasn't hers. It was
Meteor's. 'Zaria, I'm sorry I took the choice away from you,
but I . . .'

Jett. He meant the choice to save my brother or

save Feyland. Meteor had taken it out of my hands.

'No one should have to make such a decision,' he said.

I couldn't speak.

His arms lifted me and put me in the pillows of the nest. Andalonus laid my mother beside me. Her breath was weak and frantic, her eyes vacantly staring. Unlike when she first awoke from the glacier spell, she didn't seem to recognize me. I felt pain worse than being wrapped in the troll cloak. Shutting my eyes, I cried helplessly.

'*Obliv trau*,' I heard.

Opening my eyes, I saw my mother in a deep sleep.

Leona was there with her wand out. 'I'm sorry, but it had to be done, Zaree.' Her voice was more gentle than I had ever heard it.

I nodded. Cinna Tourmaline had spent five years in glacier cloth, and less than an hour after waking, what she needed most was sleep. And when she woke again, how would she bear the grief of her loss?

And how would I bear my grief? My father had been murdered before my eyes. He'd been freed from a wretched spell only because that spell protected him from the finality of death. Seeing him die wasn't any easier for having once believed him gone. If anything, it was worse to lose him twice. His last living glance had rested on me, and it haunted me now.

If I hadn't been so slow, hadn't waited endless moments, too stunned to move, he would be here in this room. Alive.

'Lily killed him to punish me for tricking her,' I mourned.

'No,' Meteor said, his green eyes watery as he leaned over me. 'She always meant to kill him.'

'I could have saved him,' I wept.

'Zaria. She baited a trap just for you.' He caressed the side of my face.

'And now she has the aevia ray, and my mother has nothing to live for.' My words ended in a sob.

Leona touched a wing to mine. 'Yes, she does.'

Andalonus hovered beside Meteor. 'You brought her home.'

'She has something to live for,' Meteor said. 'She has you.'

My friends and I gathered in the hearth room, sipping sonnia tea. I was silent, listening as they assured me that Lily would spare Jett for as long as she was unable to open the aevum derk and the aevia ray.

Too exhausted and sad to speak, I didn't voice my fear that Lily could be working with the trolls – or my knowledge that troll magic could easily open my Feynere seals. No, I didn't want to mention the trolls at all. Too well, I remembered their fortress and the crowd of them shouting, '*WE WILL HOLD YOU TO YOUR WORD.*'

The king had claimed the trolls 'took an interest' in the plight of Feyland. He had said it was no trivial battle we fought. But if he wanted to help the fey, why didn't he inflict his magic on Lily Morganite? She might be powerful, but she was still a fairy. If he could impose his magic on me – a Feynere – then surely he could impose it on her.

Rather than helping Feyland, it seemed more likely that the King of the Trolls had schemed with Lily somehow. But either way, he would soon discover I'd broken my promise to deliver the aevia ray to the rulers of Feyland. The trolls would come for me. And when they did, all the magic I had left would not help me.

I traced my wrist, my fingers stopping at my crystal watch and then opening it. The little golden hand rested on the mark just below two and a half million. I had fulfilled Lily's plans for me in so many ways, including depleting millions of radia from my reserves since the day she met me.

How would I tell my mother how much magic I had squandered? When she heard everything that had happened, would she still love me, or would she blame me for my father and Jett the way I blamed myself? And how would she take the death of Beryl Danburite, the friend she had trusted to look after me? I sat curled inside my wings, staring at the dark ash the aevum derk had left on the hearth.

'My mother,' I said to Leona. 'I didn't look at her watch. Did you? Did she drain her magic fighting the glacier cloth?'

Her expression told me the news before she spoke. 'I'm so sorry,' she said. 'Her radia is completely gone.'

* * *

Hours later, I remembered Sam Seabolt when Leona interrupted my gloomy thoughts.

'Zaree? Did you hear what I said about the human?'

'Sam?' I sat up straighter in my perch.

'Is that his name? I put him in your room under a sleep spell. I didn't know what else to do.' The new softness in Leona's voice was odd to hear but comforting. 'We should go and see him so you can tell me where to send him.'

The four of us hovered around my nest, where Sam lay like an enchanted prince, his hair a cloud of curls.

'How long till he wakes?' Andalonus asked.

'About ten more hours,' Leona said.

Andalonus pulled his ears and turned to me. 'How do you know him?'

'He's Laz's godchild, and he helped me find the comet dust.' I was telling the truth – just not all of it.

Hovering stern-faced near the door, Meteor said nothing.

Andalonus whistled. 'Laz's godchild?'

'He looks familiar,' Leona said. I was glad she didn't remember where she'd seen him before – in a room with the human who had stolen her wand. Sam didn't deserve her scorn and hatred; he'd had nothing to do with the theft.

'Why did Lily try to use him against you?' Andalonus asked curiously.

'She must have hoped she could get what she wanted,' I answered.

'But what will we do with him?' Leona touched the worn pillow next to Sam's head.

'I don't know,' I answered. 'If we send him back to his family, Lily will take him again. If we hide him somewhere on Earth, she'll fix a scope and find where he is. We can't order him to live underground the rest of his life, and I don't know how much radia it would take to conceal him for years.'

Andalonus scratched his nose. 'You could tell him the truth,' he said. 'Let *him* decide.'

'The truth?'

Andalonus shrugged. 'Maybe a spell isn't what's needed; maybe it would be wrong for *you* to decide what should happen to him. It's *his* life.'

I watched Sam's light breath, peaceful as if he slept in his own bedroom on Earth. 'I never thought of that,' I said wonderingly. 'But you're right.'

However, the thought of telling Sam all that had happened made me feel even more tired. So tired, I considered asking Leona for a sleep spell that would last at least a year.

'Our mission isn't very daunting,' said Andalonus as we left Sam to sleep. 'All we need to do is get back the crystal flask and the indigo bottle.'

'And find out what Lily and her armies are doing on Anshield Island,' Leona added.

Meteor looked at me. 'And keep Zaria safe from the trolls.'

'And find Jett,' I said quietly, floating towards the hearth room.

'It's not too much,' said Leona. 'We've already proven the four of us can work wonders.'

You're home, Mother, sleeping under a spell again, but this one is different to the nightmare you were caught in for five years. This time, a spell was cast on you because of compassion. Nothing can take away your suffering when you waken, but I hope the true rest you're getting in your own home will help at least a little.

Now that you're here, it's somehow harder for me to write to you. I pictured your arrival as joyous, not overflowing with such sorrow as this. When I began this letter, all I wanted was to find you. Now I have, but so much more has happened that I would never have foreseen.

I shiver whenever I think of Lily Morganite. By taking Father's life, and Beryl's, she has shown deeper evil than she did when she stole the magic tax from all of Feyland. She still has Jett. And now, because of me, she has both the aevum derk and the aevia ray. Also because of me, she has breached the sapphire wall on Anshield Island.

I want to make this right, Mother, and so do my friends. I could not ask for better than Leona Bloodstone, Andalonus Copper and Meteor Zircon. You knew them as children, but as you get to know them now, you will be awed by who they have become. Together, we are far more than each of us alone. Because of this, I have not lost every hope.

Even asleep, you look so fragile to my eyes, like thin glass that could easily shatter. I don't want to add to your pain, and so until I'm sure the time is right, I will keep this letter hidden away and look forward to the day your strength returns.

I will do all I can to help you, and to save Feyland.

Your fairy,

Zaria

Acknowledgments

Thank you Jessica Clarke, editor for *Indigo Magic*, for telling me what needed to be added and subtracted: Every writer knows that without magical math, a fairytale can't fly. Margaret Hope designed the beautiful cover. Writing buddies Rebecca Rowley, Lisa Pere, and Jeannie Mobley read several versions of this book and contributed helpful comments. Son Emrys used lots of humour to point out plenty of places in need of revision. Daughter Rose cheered me on and provided insights during the early stages. And husband Tim put up with all the bizarre hours I kept while communing with fairies, genies, gremlins, and trolls. Many thanks to all of you!